Praise for *How This Night Is Different*

"Elisa Albert, who's borne repeated comparisons to a budding Philip Roth, turns Passover on its head in *How This Night Is Different*—a dark, witty and incisive take on modern-day disaffected Jewish youth."

—*Variety*

"Elisa Albert offers a fresh look at being young and Jewish. . . . Her stories are edgy, daring, laced with humor and emotional complexity that's often on the dark side. Attentive to details, the 28-year-old author writes assuredly."

—*The Jewish Week*

"The greatest success of *How This Night Is Different* is its ability to be a predominantly Jewish book—exploring Jewish rituals and contemporary Jewish conundrums—while not offering the same stories over and over again. . . . Albert's protagonists are young Americans each imbued with an uncannily sharp voice, each boldly confronting their intricately conflicted lives, each looking on the world with convincing lucidity and reacting with moving joie de vivre. The fact that Albert renders these true-to-life suburbanites as meaning-seekers in front of a realistically textured cultural moment—that is Jewish— serves to strengthen each portrayal, not ghettoize it. . . . There are no clichés or stereotypes in *How This Night Is Different*, no schlemiels, no Woody Allens, no Alex Portnoys."

—*San Francisco Chronicle*

"An exceptional collection . . . the ruthless honesty and insight of Albert's prose forced me to think beyond the boxes in which her characters are often trapped. *How This Night Is*

Different is a daring book, and I can't wait to read whatever comes next."

"Instead of portraying an overwrought Jewish mother and other now-familiar Jewish stereotypes, Albert uses Judaism as a setting for mostly secular characters to air their grievances with each other or themselves."

—*The Jewish Journal*

"These 10 stories are reminiscent of Nathan Englander's purview of disaffected, disconnected, and dislocated Jews."

—*The Morning News*

"The sardonic, mischievous wit of the collection as a whole sets Albert apart from most of our celebrated young (or youngish) Jewish American women writers today. Those with a yen for bawdy, outrageous Jewish prose, prose red in tooth and claw, must turn increasingly these days to the boys—Gary Shteyngart, Nathan Englander, Jonathan Safran Foer, et al. All of which makes *How This Night Is Different,* which owes a clearer debt to Philip Roth than to Cynthia Ozick, such a refreshing contribution . . . this spirited collection heralds the arrival of an audacious new voice on the Jewish literary scene."

—*The Forward*

"Albert is a spectacularly efficient writer, able to reveal more about her characters in a few well-chosen, beautifully phrased sentences than some authors can manage in an entire novel. . . . This collection will no doubt have special resonance for Jewish readers, but its appeal doesn't stop there. The author's command of her craft should impress anyone who appreciates short fiction, and her characters are so singularly human that their power to charm and engage transcends religious affiliation. . . . An exciting debut; sincerely touching, mordantly funny and superbly assured."

—Kirkus (starred review)

"Explores traditional Jewish rituals with youthful, irreverent exuberance—hilariously vulgar."

—Publishers Weekly

"Albert's wit and insightful prose . . . allow her flawed characters to touch the reader."

—Metro

"With acid wit and bitter truth Elisa Albert rocks the High Holy House! *How This Night Is Different* is a post-modern mitzvah."

—Holiday Reinhorn, author of *Big Cats*

"Only a writer as daring as Elisa Albert would end a sharp-witted, funny, and profoundly sad debut collection with a story that yanks off the writerly mask and slashes the safety net. My jaw dropped—and not just because I was laughing."

—David Gates, author of *Jernigan*
and *The Wonders of the Invisible*
World

"Elisa Albert provides ample evidence of just how this smart, funny, outrageous young Jewish writer is different—she's wildly entertaining, incisive as an ice pick, deeply engaged, and curiously, memorably moving. Philip Roth will surely be amused and deliciously appalled, as will you, Gentle Reader, at her inheritance and renewal of the culture and the dream."

—Jayne Anne Phillips, author of *Machine*
Dreams and *MotherKind*

"How is this book different? It manages to be sharp, unflinching, tender, funny, smart, and vastly entertaining all at once. Elisa Albert's stories are a pleasure to read."

> —Tova Mirvis, author of *The Outside World*
> and *The Ladies Auxiliary*

"Elisa Albert is the real thing—funny, perceptive, quirky, and possessed of a unique voice. May she continue to write and thrive. I suspect she will have much more to tell us as the years unfold."

> —Erica Jong

"Elisa Albert is not a goody-goody. She is the wild, late-coming progeny of Philip Roth and Grace Paley, and we are lucky to have her. Her stories take contemporary Jewish life by the scruff of its neck and gives it the shaking that it deserves. There is no piety here, only what you want most from a story: hot prose and the human comedy."

> —Jonathan Wilson, author of *A Palestine Affair*

"Caustic, provocative, and completely hilarious, Elisa Albert's *How This Night Is Different* is one of the best collections I've read in a very long time."

> —Lauren Grodstein, author of
> *Reproduction Is the Flaw of*
> *Love*

"Elisa Albert spins dark comedy into gold. Smart, sexy, funny as all get-out, her stories are also profound and poignant. This is a story collection to cherish."

> —Binnie Kirshenbaum, author of
> *Hester Among the Ruins*
> and *An Almost Perfect Moment*

HOW THIS NIGHT IS DIFFERENT

Stories

ELISA ALBERT

FREE PRESS

NEW YORK   LONDON   TORONTO   SYDNEY

*f*P

FREE PRESS
A Division of Simon & Schuster, Inc.
1230 Avenue of the Americas
New York, NY 10020

First Free Press trade paperback edition February 2008

FREE PRESS and colophon are trademarks of Simon & Schuster, Inc.

For information about special discounts for bulk purchases, please contact
Simon & Schuster Special Sales at 1-800-456-6798 or business@simonandschuster.com

Designed by Joseph Rutt

"Wherever You Go" © 1983 Laurence Elis Milder

Manufactured in the United States of America
10 9 8 7 6 5 4 3 2 1

The Library of Congress has catalogued the hardcover edition as follows:
Albert, Elisa.
How this night is different: stories / Elisa Albert.
p. cm.
1. Jews—United States—Fiction. 2. Jewish women—Fiction. 3. Jewish fiction. I. Title.
PS3601.L3344 H69   2006
813'.6—dc22   2006047597

ISBN-13: 978-0-7432-9127-9
ISBN-10:   0-7432-9127-1
ISBN-13: 978-0-7432-9128-6 (pbk)
ISBN-10:   0-7432-9128-X (pbk)

For my mother and father,
Elaine and Carl

Now maybe there's a God above
but all I ever learned from love
is how to shoot at someone who outdrew you.

—Leonard Cohen, *Hallelujah*

Contents

Special bonus material at the end of the book:
Read the first chapter from Elisa Albert's forthcoming
novel *The Book of Dahlia*.

The Mother Is Always Upset

The crowd was bloodthirsty, crunching on crudités and getting antsy for some action. The eighth day after the birth, nonnegotiable, a Tuesday. Everyone had to be at work shortly.

"Let's get this show on the road, yeah?" Rich materialized next to Mark on the lip of the sunken living room and suggestively chomped the tip off a baby carrot. "Where's the kid?"

A good question. Mark, in a sleep-deprived haze, had registered the nonpresence of Beth and the baby in the living room and set about in slow motion locating them before forgetting his mission's objective in the fog of exhaustion, the lull of the din in his living room, the colorful array of vegetables and dip, the insistent pierce of his mother's voice.

"My *baby* with a *baby*!" Shirley shrieked from across the room, waving her mimosa. She was beside herself, had spent the earlier part of the morning cooing *bubbe, bubbe, bubbe* over and over again at tiny Lucas, who just stared, wide-eyed, at nothing in particular, balling his itty-bitty hands, his little hungry bird mouth ajar.

"I forgot to find them," Mark said, thinking about how the well-spaced *f*s of his response pleasantly anchored the sentiment in his *fff*-ace. He was a *fff*-ucking mess. Five hours of sleep, maybe, total, in the week since he'd become a father.

"You okay, man?" Rich offered him a hearty smack on the back, burlesque frat-boy compassion. "You look like shit."

Mark took a deep breath, cast his gaze fruitlessly about for his wife, his child. "Thanks."

"I saw Shaky McSnips-a-Lot taking a swig of the Manischewitz. I'm serious. You gonna let that guy take a knife to my nephew?"

The mohel, an elfin, gray-bearded old man, had struck in Mark an unexpected chord of affection when he'd arrived half an hour earlier to set up his little folding table and methodically lay out his gleaming tools. Now he stood by the buffet, waiting, looking vaguely lonely the way only very quiet, very compact, very old men can, starting slightly whenever Shirley busted out with one of her grandmotherly whoops of joy.

"Shut the fuck up, Rich."

"I'm just saying."

"Shut up, Rich." It felt good to Mark to have this; to have accomplished the manufacture of an entirely new person while his older brother was still paying off his condo, throwing keggers, and trying to get into the pants of C-list starlets on the Sunset Strip. Rich popped another baby carrot into his mouth and chomped on it.

"Hello, Uncle Richie," screeched Shirley, somewhat teetering over, giggling. "And Daddy Mark!" She held up her flute, knocked it back. "*L'chaim!* Where's? My? *Grandson!*"

"Hiding from the man with the cock ring and scissors, like he should be," said Rich. Mark shoved him hard, spilling the ranch dip Rich had balanced precariously on a Tostito down the front of Rich's Polo shirt. It was a thoroughly branded mess. And why were they having crudité and chips at 8:30 in the morning? Everything seemed totally off. Rich gave Mark a retaliatory shove, but a pitying, softer one. A shove that said: Yes, okay, you just fathered a child, and that's not bad, dude. Way to go.

"Boys," said Shirley. She batted her eyelashes at them, leaned in. "What do you think of Henry?" Her newest beau, a curtly self-identified "businessman" with an honest-to-goodness cowboy hat and a sparkling silver Lexus. "Cute, huh?" Shirley got even more action than Rich.

"Mom, why don't you lay off the champagne for a while?"

Shirley was wearing a too-tight, too-bright, too-low, turquoise V-neck, her bony excuse for cleavage fairly heaving. Mark felt suddenly like the father of everyone in the room, of everyone in the world. The desire to simply lie down on the floor and close his eyes crashed like a wave over him.

"Sandy Weinstein wants to know what a nice Jewish baby is doing with a name like *Lucas*," Shirley offered, her voice low and conspiratorial. "She said: 'Lucas. How very New Testament.' I told her the real right-wing Christians are Israel's best friend these days and to just shove it." At this she cackled happily. She'd bristled a bit herself when she first heard the name, naturally, but had been happy they'd picked an *L* name, at least, for Lou.

"Mom, it's Lev, in Hebrew, for Dad." Lou Roth had been dead now some twenty-five years. Testicular cancer at thirty-eight, poor man. But it was the kind of father loss that had been a bigger deal for the vacuum it had created. Mark didn't really remember his father's death as a particularly traumatic event. He and Rich had simply been spirited away to relatives for a period of weeks. It was more the lack that resonated, the absence of Lou that loomed largest. The guy simply was never and had never been around.

Beth had hoped to name the baby after her grandmother Rose, who'd managed to escape the Nazis and achieve low-grade fame for a thin volume of poetry spared proper criticism only for the import of its historical context. But in the end the specter of Lou had won out in the tragedy tug-of-war. He was cut down in his prime, hadn't gotten to see his kids grow up, had been robbed of his life: Mark played it to the hilt. Grandma Rose had lived a long life and met eight grandchildren, *three* of whom were already named for her. The Holocaust notwithstanding, Lou was the clear winner. They pondered Leonard, Lew, Lawrence, Lance, and settled eventually on Lucas because Beth had known a guy in high school who went by Luke and was, as she put it, a total hottie. Lev would be trotted out ceremoniously once in a while, starting today; for Lucas's bar mitzvah, his wedding, his eventual funeral.

"Well," said Shirley. "He's healthy, is all that matters. *I* certainly don't care that he's named after an apostle. He's got ten fingers and toes, is all."

"And soon he won't have a foreskin," Rich said, pleased with himself. They squinted at him.

4

Mark took a deep breath, clamped his hands over his face, and rubbed vigorously. "O-kay," he said, slapping his cheeks with both palms like in an after-shave commercial. "Yes, indeedy. Okay. All right. Conversation for another time."

In the kitchen, where Beth also wasn't, an ash blond with a streaked mullet grabbed Mark by the arm. She had a small pacifier tattooed on the inside of her wrist, poking out from under a leather cuff. Mark caught himself staring at the pacifier, the way it seemed nestled in the softest, loveliest spot imaginable, near a plump vein, and quickly looked away. The beginnings of an erection stirred in his pants. On the fridge behind them, Beth's KEEP ABORTION LEGAL sticker loomed large, like a grinning face. This exhaustion resembled nothing so much as an acid trip he'd taken the summer after college, everything shifty and fluid, everything itself at first giving way to other things, which themselves became the things, and so on.

"Where is she?"

"Hi," he said, sticking out a tired hand. "I'm Mark."

"Kimberly. You know me. From the group." Ah, yes. Shit. Beth's natural-childbirth-slash-new-moms' support group.

"Right," he said. "Hey."

The group had been central to Beth's pregnancy; she'd prattled on endlessly about this one's polycystic ovaries and that one's idiot sister's awful scheduled C-section. "Birth is not a medical problem," they all repeated, mantra-style, at the end of every meeting. "Birth is a natural process." Beth went once a week to work on visualization exercises, talk about the sacred space new moms need to create for themselves, and get the dirt on the best doulas in town. There had been a virgin cocktail party in Beth's sixth month, all the women either expecting or breast-feeding, and Mark had made himself quite unpopular by wondering aloud whether the men couldn't possibly have a beer or two. It wasn't like *they* were pregnant. Except, as Beth made clear in the car on the way home, hissing at him, the *least* an expectant father could do was behave as if he were pregnant, too. What was the matter with him? He had embarrassed her, he had embarrassed himself.

"You think this is fun?" she had said, gesturing down at her giant belly where the seat belt cut into it. "You think I don't want a glass of wine? You think we're all *comfortable*?" He had, actually, assumed she was comfortable. It was a natural process, after all, right? He'd thought about and sort of envied her the space inside her that had been empty and now was full. She looked like a painting, all aglow. When he told her as much, she'd snorted.

"Yeah, Mark, I'm happy as a clam. I have no ankles and my butt is leaking and I can't eat sushi. Thank you s o much for knocking me up. This is pretty much the nexus of my female existence, and I owe it all to you."

Hormones, Mark told himself. All the pregnancy books, the what-to-expect-when-your-wife-is-expecting books, spoke forebodingly about the hormones. It had become his own mantra: hormones, hormones, hormones. Faith that she meant very little of what she said during those months became a kind of religion for him.

When she freaked out about unwashed dishes, screaming and crying about how she couldn't possibly do everything herself and how was she supposed to take care of *two* babies, let alone the one she was about to have, Mark just apologized and hugged her, thinking: hormones. When she went to stay at her mother's for a week in her seventh month, unsure if she "really wanted to share the parenting of this child" with him, he just rode it out, smiled, bought her a pregnancy massage gift certificate, pretended everything was normal.

He cultivated the notion that she really did love him, love being pregnant, love the imminence of motherhood, despite the fact that in the face of her hostility those things seemed about as likely as creationism.

Kimberly was looking at him as though it was entirely possible he had duct-taped Beth in the basement and fed the baby to the dog.

"So where is she?" Ah, yes, it was all coming back to him now. How could he forget? This was *Kimberly*, whose partner, Lynda, was having a sperm donor's baby. A six-foot-one sperm donor with blond hair and green eyes, an IQ of 175, and no family history of cancer or heart disease, Beth had relayed dreamily to him after group one week. She'd affected the sigh of a twelve-year-old opening up the centerfold in *Teen Beat*, seized by lust for the perfect genetic makeup. Oh, Mark, she'd said to him, eyes glazed over. Can you imagine? Can you even imagine what a gorgeous baby they're going to have?

"I'm going to find her," he said, not quite used to the fact that where Beth had once been a single person she had now split off into two. Every time he blinked he had to pry his eyelids apart again. Please, his brain wept. Just a little rest. Just a few seconds. A minute. He attempted brightness. "We gotta get this show on the road, right?"

Kimberly stared at him in disgust. Kimberly, whose partner, Lynda, was giving birth to a hardy little Hitler youth. Kimberly, who for the past six months had given Beth nonstop shit about the barbarism of the particular ritual they were gathered here to watch performed on their child by the small and trembling man conspicuously, thankfully, not holding a mimosa.

"She doesn't want to do this, you know," Kimberly said to him.

"What?"

"She doesn't want to do this. You've pushed her into it, and she doesn't want to do it. It's a really fucked-up ritual. There's no medical reason to subject Lucas to something so painful and invasive." She hooked her thumbs into her belt loops and jutted out a hip, pleased with herself, Mark thought, for blowing her sanctimonious wad. It did nothing, truth be told, to diminish his half-inflated boner. "It's incredibly selfish of you to push your religious beliefs onto an infant."

"Kimberly? Thanks. I think we disagree. Let's not get into this."

She shook her head. "Whatever. The least you could've done, if you really, like, *needed* to surgically alter his penis, is do it at the hospital. Instead of in some barbaric, public act where we're all supposed to stand around and cheer or whatever."

He was about to say something jocular along the lines of 'Lady, relax! Look at me! I turned out okay!' but decided in the nick (tee-hee) of time that it was not a good idea to reference his own ritually circumcised member. Had he, in fact, turned out okay? In high school he'd developed a mortifying fondness for some not-quite-mainstream porn, hiding it under his bed, where it glowed shamefully red and hot like coal until, inevitably, Shirley had found it. He'd gotten gonorrhea in college, passed it on to a girlfriend who'd furiously broken up with him after warning most of her friends and their friends, effectively destroying any chance he had to sleep with half the girls in his class. He'd loved—truly, deeply—the woman before Beth and for no good reason had fucked her best friend. He'd impregnated Beth a few months before their wedding, necessitating a prenuptial abortion that had so upset her she almost backed out of the marriage. One could argue that he had not, in fact, turned out okay. One could say that he'd actually Darth Vadered his dick a bit over the years, used its powers for evil rather than good. And now there was this matter of passing down its shape and purpose to the new person he'd created with it.

He played his only trump card. "Listen, Kimberly, we know how you feel about this. But it's a religious matter, and it's highly personal, so." Ha-ha. Take that, goyishe dyke. "I'm going to find Beth. She's probably feeding him or something," he said as he turned down the hall, self-conscious that he sounded characteristically, necessarily, detached from that process. Kimberly and Lynda, with the help of a cash-strapped Nazi jerking off to a dog-eared *Hustler,* would gladly evolve his sorry, balding, five-nine-with-genetic-disease-eating-away-at-his-entire-family-tree ass right out of the picture and be no worse off for it.

"Whatever," she said to his back. "His penis is going to look *just like yours.* How special for you."

Coming out of the bathroom, Mark's once beloved, corruptive older cousin Michael zipped up his fly. "Is this happening

9

soon, man? 'Cause I gotta be at a meeting in the valley at ten." Michael worked for a media conglomerate referred to by Beth as "Satan Incorporated." He'd hired a half dozen strippers to show up at Mark's otherwise entirely tame bachelor party and had been excoriated by Beth, who'd found out. It had been the definitive end to a mentor relationship that, at one time, had filled the void left first by Lou dying and then by Rich turning out to be such a total douche.

"Very soon. Need find baby. Then start."

Michael pressed his palms together and bowed at the hips.

"Ah, yes, Markus-san. Need baby boy before penis ritual can proceed." He raised a fist into the air. "Find me baby boy!" he boomed, and cracked himself up.

"Working on it," Mark said. Michael went into the kitchen and gave Kimberly the once-over. *'Sup?*

Beth was not in the living room. Beth was not in the kitchen. Beth was not in the hallway or the bathroom. This, their first house, bought with a thirty-year mortgage and loans from both Shirley and Beth's parents, was not in theory actually large enough to warrant such a lengthy search. Mark poked his head into the master bedroom, with its tapestry over the bed and the four-foot-tall bong stashed in the back of the closet.

"Don't you think maybe it's time for a design overhaul?" Beth had said to him some months ago, lying on the bed, just beginning to show.

"Why?" he'd asked, innocently enough.

"Because, Mark. I'm about to have a *child,* here. Do you get that? There's going to be another person here, who we're responsible for. We're, like, bringing someone into the world, and it's our job not to fuck this person up completely. Do you get that?" Here she'd started sobbing uncontrollably.

"Sweetie, sure. It's fine. Don't worry. We can do whatever you want." Hormones, hormones, right.

She had gesticulated wildly at the tapestry, the IKEA bookshelves. "It's like a fucking dorm room in here. This is totally insane. We can't bring a *person* into the world. What the *fuck*, Mark?" She'd buried her face in a pillow, impervious to Mark's attempts to soothe her. Hormones, hormones, hormones.

Sandee Stern (graduate of Stanford, resident of Silverlake, school social worker, wife of Stew, and Mark's favorite of the group because of her entirely alliterated life), was sitting on their bed, breast-feeding one-month-old Sophie.

"Hi, Daddy!" she said, before he could duck back out into the hall. The perversity of anyone really calling him this, even in jest, gave him fucking chills, actual chills, shooting up and down his spine. "Has the deed been done?"

"No," he told her. "Not yet. We're missing a key player."

At the end of the hall, the door to the nursery (until three months before, the "office") was closed. Bingo.

"Beth?" He knocked twice. Nothing.

From the living room, Shirley: "Yesterday! I could swear Mark's bris was *yesterday*. Where does the time go? I know! And now I'm a *grandma*!" He could well picture her expression as she did this bit; eyes wide, painted lips stretched tight around laser-whitened teeth. Henry would be next to her, his arm around her waist just lasciviously enough to look off, fingers brushing against the top of her ribs and the bottom of her tits under the too-tight shirt. "Not the most well-endowed," Shirley had confided in Mark a few weeks earlier, "but he's very tender with me in bed."

"Mom," he'd begged. "Please. Please."

Mark pressed his fingertips against the hollow plywood door, his forehead against the rough, unpainted surface of it. The lightbulb in the fixture overhead had gone out a few days earlier, but changing it had not exactly been high on either Mark or Beth's list of priorities. It was not an entirely terrible place to take a nap. He let himself close his eyes briefly, just to experience the sheer ecstasy of it. What a gift to flip the switch of that one measly sense.

"Beth?" he found the energy to ask thinly. "Hey. Sweetie?"

He tried the knob. Locked.

"Everything is okay?" The mohel, behind him. Pronounced *moil* by Shirley, like *foil, soil, boil, recoil.* He was eighty if he was a day, but came highly recommended by the temple sisterhood as *the* foreskin obliterator in town. A *fourth-generation* mohel, according to Shirley. This, apparently, was like the Eastern European equivalent of being a Kennedy.

Mark turned around, nodded slightly. "Yes, fine." Not having had a father for most of his life had made Mark sort of nervous around older men; a combination of amazement that any man should actually live past forty, disgust that they might want to screw his mom, and longing for a game of catch in the yard, company on an imagined, retroactive pre–bar mitzvah trip to a brothel.

"The baby is okay?"

"I—yes. We'll start soon, sir." He did this around men old enough to be his father: stood up straight, patted down his figurative cowlicks. The way orphans behave in foster care, hopeful that clean fingernails and good manners will earn them a permanent home.

"I have this for you," the mohel said, producing from a folder a few stapled pages. "After Care," read the top sheet. There were bullets, bold type, a small diagram. Mark tasted bile. He folded the packet decisively in half.

"Thank you."

"You will call me if you have any questions, yes? My phone number is on the top."

"Yes," Mark said. "Thank you."

The mohel smiled, followed Mark's gaze toward the closed door. "The mother is upset?"

"I don't know," Mark whispered.

"It is not unusual," the mohel said. "It is very common." Mark nodded.

"Do you want for me to speak with her?"

Yes, he thought. "No, it's okay. Everything is fine."

Rich came down the hallway and stepped into the bathroom. He looked at the mohel, Mark, the door.

"Probably giving him a pep talk," he said, leering out against the doorframe. He made a minimegaphone out of his hands and hollered into it. "Be brave, little man!"

"Shut *up,* you dick!" Mark said, with more force than he thought he could muster. The word "dick" hung in the air, an apropos pejorative. "My brother," he added, apologetically, when Rich had closed the door.

"Yes," said the mohel. "He is the *sandak*?" The honored relative who was to hold the baby during the ceremony. Usually a grandfather, but in this case, given the dearth of multigenerational males in the Roth family, yes, sadly, Rich.

13

"The baby is named for our father," Mark said, nodding. "Lev."

"Ah," said the old man, beaming. He put his hand to his chest. "Heart. A beautiful name."

Why had they named him in both English and Hebrew? Lucas seemed suddenly like the most superfluous, strange name Mark had ever heard. Almost as strange right then as Lou, that mysterious, shadowy figure. A guy so nice they named him twice, Mark singsonged to himself, swaying and senseless, exhausted.

Endless streams of overwrought baby announcements had been arriving constantly from Beth and Mark's starter yuppie friends over the past few years. And oh, Christ, the *names!* What were people thinking? They'd laughed maliciously at the repetitive Jacobs and Emmas, the trashy Skylars, the ludicrous Dakotas. You could tell a lot about people from their name choices. Their class aspirations, their delusions. The people they themselves had wanted to be but failed.

"How many ways," Beth would wonder aloud, fingering heavy Italian paper threaded intricately with either pink or blue ribbon, "could there possibly be to euphemize this?" *Oh, Boy— Molly has a brother! Jamie would like to announce the arrival of his parents! Sugar and Spice and Everything Nice, Twice: Samantha and Stacey have arrived!* She'd fantasized about one that would say: *Beth and Mark, who like to do it doggie-style, somehow replicated themselves in a Brand New Person (!), who was born shortly after 7 a.m. on August 18, after Beth, in a kind of pain she can best try to describe in interpretive dance, was forced to abandon her birth plan of squatting in a whirlpool and eschewing the horrid medicalization thrust so often upon inno-*

cent, *healthy women in delivery, was heavily anesthetized and had her genitalia ripped to shreds while Mark stood by and said things like, "You're doing great, honey."* And with yellow ribbon, definitely, or green or purple, for fuck's sake; none of that archaic gender color-ghettoizing for *their* little *schmoopie-woopie-head.*

"I don't know if that'll go over so well with the nice folks who've been buying us stuff off our baby registry, darlingest," Mark had said. They'd ended up doing one that said, simply: Lucas Wein-Roth (Mark had won the extremely heated coin toss—two out of three—and therefore gotten Roth last) printed in large type, with the relevant pound/ounce/date info below, and for delighted contrarian effect, a footnoted "No gendered gifts, please." Lev was nowhere to be seen, because why transliterate it? And why confuse people unfamiliar with the Hebrew?

The mohel stood in silence by the door for a few seconds. Mark knocked again, inspired to take further action, however futile, if only for the mohel's benefit. "Beth. Honey, I know this is upsetting. Please open up." He looked at the mohel for a thumbs-up or something.

"The mother is always upset," the mohel said quietly. He giggled. "If God had asked Abraham to remove some skin from his knee and the knees of all the males in his household, it would be probably not so difficult."

Mark pondered this for a moment. The mother, always upset. Hormones, whatever: This was how it would be now. It was a warning; it was a heads-up. He would file this information away alongside cautionary tales of men twisted up in jealousy of their sons' commandeering of breasts and motherly attention, alongside Rich-given wisdom about the merits of anal sex postchildbirth.

"Babe, the mohel is here. It's time to start." His voice was teetering upward desperately. For a split second he thought he might just break the goddamn door down and be done with it. A burst of pure hatred for her (for having been the one to bear this boy and for keeping him behind this door and for keeping him from this rite that connected him directly back to the beginning of Jewish fucking time) shot into his heart as if from a syringe.

"Allow me," said the mohel. He stepped up to the door as if it were a podium of some kind, a pulpit. "Hello, Beth. This is Rabbi Trager. I would like very much to speak to you for a few moments, please." He said "Beth" like "bet."

And sure enough, after a beat, there was a click, the swoosh of opening, and the mohel was gone, swallowed up in the room. The door clicked shut again behind him. As easy as that. Like what he'd once upon a time imagined birth to be. Mark stood in the hall, alone again under the fixture with the dead bulb. In the living room, he heard his cousin Michael saying good-bye, explaining to Shirley about the meeting in the valley at ten, then clapping Rich on the back and saying something about not really wanting to see the poor little dude get his johnson cut anyhow. Mark wondered what was happening in the nursery, what the mohel could possibly be saying to his angry and sleep-deprived wife to make her relax her grip on their son and offer him up to the gaping maw of a tradition that excluded her.

Shirley appeared wild eyed in the hall. "People are leaving!" she said. "What's going on?"

Mark didn't respond. He pressed the back of his skull into the wall and kept his eyes resolutely shut. Beth despised

Shirley, had nicknamed her AstroGlide and tried often to joke with Mark about what a desperately hypersexual sixty-five-year-old skank she was. This took the form of many pointed "your mother" jokes, which Beth found utterly hilarious.

"Mark!"

"Mom."

"Mark!!"

"Mom."

Shirley seemed then miraculously to understand that Mark was not in charge, had no way of making happen what was supposed to happen. That he needed to close his eyes and lean against the wall in that dark spot of the hallway, as close as he could get to his wife, his child. She left him there and went back out into the living room. He never loved her more in all his life.

"A few minutes, everyone," she said. "They just need a few more minutes."

When the mohel emerged from the nursery with baby Lucas/Lev in his arms, Mark started awake. Had it been a minute? An hour?

"The mother is of course upset, but she understands that it is important," the mohel said. "She says she cannot watch it, and she apologizes for making a problem."

The baby fidgeted a little and closed his eyes. Oh, Beth. He was such a selfish prick.

"The mother is always upset," said the mohel. "It is normal."

Mark looked at the mohel. "Really? It's normal?"

The mohel chuckled, cradling the baby expertly. "Yes. Always. Always."

This was an incredible relief, really. Mark stood there under the dark fixture with the mohel, gazing at Lucas. Like a little family, the three of them.

They had put a framed picture of Lou on the table, with a shit-eating grin, huge seventies glasses frames, and a faded orangey tint. He looked like a big man up there, Mark thought, pleased as punch with the way life had carried on without him, with his new namesake and his plum VIP spot for watching this little latter-day Lev be welcomed into the covenant.

Per the mohel's instructions, Mark dipped his index finger into the sticky-sweet red wine and then put it gently into Lucas's mouth. Rich ambled up to the front of the room and took his place next to Mark, hands folded over his crotch like a mafioso. A hush fell over the crowd. No one seemed to miss Beth. It was perfectly acceptable somehow that this baby boy had sprung forth from Mark alone, from the smiling picture of Lou, from Rich, from flavor-of-the-month Henry in his ridiculous cowboy hat, from the old man addressing them all.

"The *orlah*," the mohel began, "or foreskin, is a metaphor for any barrier in the heart of a man which would prevent him from hearing God, understanding God." Kimberly, standing with Lynda at the back of the room, could be heard loudly expelling air from her nostrils. *Metaphor, my ass.*

Shirley had wanted someone to speak about Lou, about the kind and generous man he had been, about how these qualities would hopefully be passed down to his grandson along with his name. So Mark, with the baby asleep in his arms, moved to the front of the table.

"My father was a special man," he began. "A very special man." Someone coughed. "And we wanted to honor him by giving Lucas his name." For what he could remember of his father and a dollar, Mark could probably get a soda.

Mark placed his son gently into Rich's arms (oh, God, man, pretend he's a football, and please don't fucking drop him). And then the onesie was being peeled off, the diaper removed to reveal those insanely huge infant balls and the perky little penis nub that looked so foreign (not for long) to Mark.

There was more talk, a blessing or two. Mark concentrated on breathing, on not passing out. "Behold!" the mohel read from a book. "A man loves no one better than his son, and yet he circumcises him!"

And then there was a flurry of metal, the snip, a beat, a gut-wrenching wail from Lucas, and a chorus of "Mazel tov!"'s that went up like flame around the room. Easy as that.

"Ouch," said Rich, staring intently at the fascinating source of Lucas's pain.

Before he left, the mohel handed Mark a folded cloth napkin, a little pouch.

"Bury it," he said. "In your yard. As soon as possible."

So when everyone had finally gone home—"No more visitors for the child today," ordered the mohel—and the baby had been given a bottle and fallen asleep in his crib—"Quickest-forgotten pain in the world," said Shirley, Henry leading her out the door with his hand on her ass—Mark went out to the yard with a shovel he found in the garage and dug a hole. It didn't need to be too deep, he figured, just so long as a neighborhood dog wouldn't come sniffing around and dig the thing up for a snack in the next few days. He dropped the napkin in, covered it over with dirt, and patted it down. He imagined briefly that he would have a hard time forgetting this spot, even after lots and lots of time had passed. It was like a grave, or, no: It was like the opposite of a grave. His hands were dirty when he was done, and he liked the way it felt. He was conscious of feeling, somehow, absurdly, like a man. Then he went back inside to clean up.

Once everything was more or less back in place, the folding chairs folded, the lipstick-ringed paper napkins trashed, Mark knocked softly on the bedroom door and entered without a word. Beth was curled up on her side of the bed, facing away from him. Was she sleeping? Should he wake her? How could he upset her least? He stood looking at her back for a long moment, terrified of doing or saying the wrong thing, afraid even of his own breath, which escaped anyway. But he supposed he knew the score now, knew that it didn't much matter what he did or said or didn't do or didn't say. He sat down on the bed.

"Hi," Beth said, turning over to look at him, her eyes watery and wide.

"I wanted a girl," he said.

When You Say You're a Jew

The taxi driver, like everyone else in Lisbon, correctly assumes that Debra is American (blond, check; fanny pack, check; look of entitlement, check) and speaks to her accordingly, in English. "Where to?" he demands when she gets into his cab in the Praca de Republica.

Debra, embarrassed by her monolinguality, tries to respond in Portuguese. *"Para Rua Las Palmas,"* she says haltingly. Her phrase book is dog-eared, limp and ragged as a child's doll, and Debra clings to it as fiercely and superstitiously.

The driver, an excitable middle-aged man with a unibrow and arms sleeved in black hair, has no patience for tourists and their phrase books, so he just holds out his hand for the map, takes a brief look at it, and puts the car in gear. *"Para a synagogua,"* he says.

"Si."

Out the window she watches the city rush by and begin to thin out. Are there speed limits here? She digs around in the folds of the backseat for a seat belt but gives up when her

21

hand comes into contact with something wet and cold. By virtue of being en route to a synagogue, she hopes, they will not crash.

"American?"

"*Si.*" Debra has been in Portugal for two weeks now, on vacation, traveling by herself.

"Ahhhh," he says, as if he approves, "American!"

"I'm Jewish," she tells him. Debra is many things (American, bisexual, dog lover, Neil Young fan) but chiefly, at this moment, whittled down by solitary travel in a foreign country and slightly scared for her life in the backseat of a barreling càb, she is, most certainly, a Jew. She can feel it in her bones, the way, around twelve, she'd arrive at sleepover camp armed to the teeth with a whole new persona, different from the Debra she'd been all year at school, ready to act out an entirely new side of herself. This is Camp Shalom and I am Good At Sports and Popular (not the least bit Likely to Cry When Teased About My Excessive Blushing). This is Lisbon, Portugal, and I am a Jew (not at all, mind you, just Another Aimless Ethnocentric Postcollegiate Traveler).

The taxi driver nods lazily and offers her an encouraging please-tip-me-well smile in the rearview mirror. Debra clutches the phrase book to her breast, wondering if there is enough time left in the ride for the piecing together of any sort of pseudo-meaningful conversation in Portuguese. She longs for a friendly exchange with the taxi driver, as with any number of random people—the man who sold her her metro ticket Wednesday afternoon, the woman who sold her a stack of postcards on the Rua Augusta the day before—she's encountered on her lonely journey. But no, she reminds herself, invoking the wisdom of the tersely worded Women Traveling Alone section of her tour book, being a *lone* woman traveler is not the same as being a *lonely* woman traveler. She is the former, yes, but it is up to her whether or not she will become the latter. She is a Jew in a far-flung locale on her way to a synagogue on Friday evening, and so in this way she is a lone traveler, but certainly not a lonely one. *Brava,* she tells herself.

There had been the churches, sure, everywhere she went: towering monstrosities for which she could not muster anything more than vague architectural appreciation. There were the ruins of a Moorish castle in Sintra, where she stood high up on a boulder, hands on hips, and, rattling fear of heights notwithstanding, declared herself ruler of all she surveyed. And in Sagres she'd even reached the "end of the world," the southwesternmost tip of Europe, a vantage point from which it was much easier to believe the world was indeed flat, all evidence to the contrary. The wind had been extraordinary, coming off those couple of thousand miles of unbroken ocean and painfully whipping her hair against her face, and she'd sat on a rock and screamed her name into it, unable to hear herself.

But when Debra saw the synagogue listed in the index of her tour book (Worship, Places of) she felt a tug inside her, like a lightbulb with a chain. She wanted to see this place, one of two synagogues left in Portugal, once a thriving center of Jewish life. She wanted to be infused by its living, breathing presence. How miraculous, she thinks in the cab, humming the Inquisition song from Mel Brooks's *History of the World*—"The Inquisition, what a show! The Inquisition, here we go!"—to be alive and well and affluent and Jewish in such a place.

She's slightly concerned that it will be a different sort of synagogue, somehow, the way that children believe that dogs from different countries will bark in different languages. She wonders if Friday-night services will resemble those at home—the pretty melodies, overdose-of-perfume nausea, and chocolate lace cookies of her religious upbringing—and simultaneously hopes so and not, as she has no model for imagining anything different but has no particular fondness for the aforementioned assault on the senses.

They drive into a suburb, and from the backseat of the slowed taxi Debra almost mistakes the synagogue for another of the two-story family homes that line the block, but a large wrought-iron Star of David flush above the door gives it away. And then she sees the small Hebrew letters spelling out *Tifereth Israel*. Of course: why had she been worried she wouldn't recognize it? Hebrew is Hebrew, no matter what country it's in, and Debra is the product of a compulsory Hebrew school education, twice weekly after school from the sixth grade through the twelfth. Here is Hebrew, and she can read it. She leans forward in her seat, flipping through her phrase book for the way to say, "Slow down, please, stop right here."

"Aqui, esta bem," she says, "That's fine, right here," when she finds "here" in the English-Portuguese section of the phrase book, sandwiched between "herbs" (*as ervas*) and "hers" (*dela*). It's a good phrase book, not just a glorified dictionary. It groups words together contextually, cross-references, sports on its cover a picture of a sun-dappled fish-

24

ing boat moored on a sandy beach, calms her. "Confidence goes a long way when speaking a foreign language," says the introduction.

The driver slams on the brakes, and Debra, minus seat belt, is thrown against the front seat like a limbed sack of grain. She's been writing amused postcards home about the apparent lack of litigiousness in European society. No fences or bars around castle turrets, no CAUTION: HOT on the sides of disposable coffee cups. No seat belts in cabs. This might otherwise have felt liberating, but Debra is a Woman Traveling Alone, and she feels constantly in danger of some potentially fatal lapse in common sense.

"I like the Jim Carrey," the driver tells her as she's rooting through her bag for six euros to pay him. She is touched by this bit of cultural outreach, knows what effort is involved with putting together thoughts with unfamiliar words.

"*Obrigada,*" she says to him, *thank you,* as if she herself, as a representative from America, is responsible for the Jim Carrey. She means to thank him for many things: the ride, his comment on American comedic ingenuity, his attempts to communicate with her in her own language. Debra prides herself on her convincing rendition of *obrigada,* the *r* rolled and the *da* a "the." She has, actually, been surprised and pleased by the myriad uses there seem to be for this word. "Thank you" she took for granted. *Obrigada* could be used a hundred times a day for anything from a greeting to a sarcastic retort. It is her only surefire Portuguese word, and she uses it constantly, with great affection.

The driver giggles to himself, perhaps reliving a funny Jim

Carrey moment. Debra is herself rather partial to Jim Carrey but has no way of communicating this, so the opportunity for bonding is moot. She gives him the euros, which seem like Monopoly money, and he accelerates before she's even closed the door, mid-*Obrigada*.

It occurs to Debra, listening to his engine fade away, that she is potentially screwed. Alone in a quiet suburb with no way to get back to the city, to the old woman with the chin hair who runs her *pensão*. Debra stands on the wide, paved street in front of the synagogue and invents a worst-case scenario in which she will have to knock on the door of a house and ask to use a phone. Would that make her an unwise lone-woman traveler? What would a *Let's Go* writer do? This is her fail-safe bumper-sticker question, and over the past few weeks she's winnowed it down to a partially familiar acronym: WWALGWD?

The synagogue seems closed up, like a summer home in winter. Or a winter home in summer. Like an out-of-season home, at any rate. The front gate is locked. Debra mock-rattles it with her fists closed around two iron stems. There is a bell, the kind that glows weakly until you press it, when instantly the small light within is put out. She presses it, and a clanging ring echoes on the block. The stylish houses and well-groomed shrubbery do not flinch. Given that it's Friday night, the start of the Sabbath, the quiet is disconcerting.

At home, at the synagogue to which Debra's family has always belonged but only sporadically attended, the expansive parking lot is a hub of pre-*Shabbes* activity and gossip. It had been in that parking lot, accosted by a group of squawking sisterhood ladies, that a twelve-year-old Debra had found out

26

her mother was a convert. "Debra! Such a gorgeous girl! That blond hair! Our little *shiksa!*"

She had, of course, gone straight to her parents, who were talking to another couple in the lobby. *What's a* shiksa?

A sit-down with the rabbi had been arranged. He was a young, liberal, recent seminary grad. A few years later he got himself fired for performing a gay commitment ceremony.

"Debra," he had said to her in his small, wood-paneled office. "Your mother is Jewish and your father is Jewish, and that means that you are a Jew." She had nodded obediently, nurturing the first, bright green shoots of a massive crush on him. "When someone decides they want to become Jewish, like your mom did, they become a hundred percent Jewish."

"Okay," Debra had said. He had dimples.

"And you know what?" the rabbi had continued, "It's against Jewish law even to point out that someone decided to become Jewish instead of being born Jewish. Mrs. Weinstein was really wrong to mention it."

"Mmm-hm," she'd replied. Let's see, in ten years she'd be twenty-two and he'd be—well, who knew, like, forty? It was doable.

"In fact," he'd continued, in full earnest young clergyman mode, "people who choose to be Jewish are in a way even *more* Jewish than those who are born into it. Because, see, they had to make the *choice,* and that means a lot. That's how completely someone becomes Jewish when they convert."

Oh! That word! "Convert." Debra had been seized with it. It was a word for a butterfly coming out of a cocoon, an intonation for a chemical transaction in which a thing magically

27

becomes something else. It seemed fantastical in noun form, a wonderful thing to have gone through, infinitely preferable to the recently bandied-about "puberty." A convert. Her mother was one. The implications were lovely.

Debra rings the bell again. A superego ticker-tape commentary runs in her inner ear: *You didn't call first? You have no idea where you are? What a fucking idiot. Who does this?* It occurs to her that her superego is made up of all the people she's ever known, in chorus. She wonders if this is already accepted psychology dogma or if she's just made a breakthrough in the field. People were probably always making commonsense breakthroughs in disciplines totally foreign to them; the world's ills had probably already been solved in secret isolation.

She begins casing the nearby houses to decide which most likely contains the least lascivious xenophobe when the door of the synagogue swings open. A woman in a complexly patterned black-and-white muumuu waddles out halfway.

"No!" she says, all knit brow and muumuu. She waves Debra away. *"Desculpe!"*

"Hola! Obrigada!" Debra offers, thereby exhausting her applicable Portuguese. "Hey."

The woman sighs deeply, the demonstration for aliens from a far-off planet of what it is to be *at the end of one's rope.* "No, no, no," she says. *"Fechado. Desculpe."*

The central fault of phrase books is that the patience to comb through them is completely eradicated when one is in the thick of an exchange during which a phrase or two might be helpful. "Hey, wait! Um . . ."

The woman gives in. She and her flower pattern make their way down to the gate.

"*Obrigada*," Debra calls out to the woman as she approaches, hoping this conveys a sort of apology for being a bother, for being a foreigner, for ringing the bell twice, for not knowing how to speak the language of the country she's in.

The woman does not open the gate. "*De-scul-PE!*"

"*Hel-lo*," Debra says. "I am A-mer-ican, I am *traveling*. I want to come to *Shabbat* services. I am sorry that I am wearing these *shoes*," she gestures down at her flip-flops, a pretty universal house-of-worship fashion no-no.

The woman looks Debra over disapprovingly. Debra imagines the woman is taking in her blondness, her thinly lashed green eyes, her button nose. Debra's face is a billboard of freedom and fearlessness, a map of ease and rule. If she's heard it once, she's heard it a thousand times: *You don't* look *Jewish*. Jews look more like this woman: swarthy and Cimmerian; unlit. Not like Debra, on whom the sun seems always to have been shining.

If this were the fifteenth century, Debra would be golden. No need to have her fingernails torn off, the soles of her feet scorched: Look at her! We know what she is! In Evora she'd sipped iced tea high up on a hill, at the ruins of a Roman temple, which her tour book said had served as a site of public Inquisition rites. Scores of people, the dumb ones who didn't get out, forced into conversion or killed. *Conversos*, they were called. The country was full of them, all good, forgetful Christians generations later. Some families, she'd read, had held on to random traditions without even knowing why. They'd clung steadfastly to a refusal to eat pork over hundreds of years: because my mother didn't eat pork, because her mother didn't eat pork, and so on. Debra had struck up a conversation with a man in a *pastelaria* in Porto who told her his mother lit two candles every Friday night of her life. No blessing, no meaning, no clue why she did it, just satisfaction with the imperative that she do it. Friday night was candle night. Just because it had always been that way. Also there were the *Marranos,* who kept Torahs buried beneath their houses, educated their children by candlelight, went to church like good converts but observed the laws of Judaism secretly, underground. *Marranos,* meaning pigs. Though apparently eventually most of these just faded out; exhausted, scared, lonely, all the things religion is supposed to prevent.

You don't look Jewish. Usually it is a compliment, delivered with a swagger by some would-be suitor. They can hardly contain their excitement; she is a treasure, a trophy, the mythical blond Semite, a unicorn. *And you don't look stupid,* she always wishes she could spit back, so huge is her rage at the falsity her face seems always to be trumpeting.

When, in the ninth grade, *The Diary of Anne Frank* was chosen as the school play, Debra figured that she, as one of only a handful of Jews in her class, would be a shoo-in for the lead. Hadn't she read the book *twice,* and cried each time? Wasn't she prohibited to go out on Friday nights because of her mother's mandatory attendance policy at family Shabbat dinners? It seemed only natural that she should be the one called upon to channel the spirit of her beloved Anne; a deserved right, a sort of reparation, if you will, that the drama teacher at Taft Junior High was beholden to perform. When the role went to Cindy *Torricelli,* an Italian girl with dark, sunken eyes and virtually no forehead, Debra had been devastated. Cindy *Torricelli,* for God's sake, who wore a chintzy gold *cross* around her neck that she refused to take off even during the performances, when she insisted on tucking it into her shirt instead. This was an insult to the entire Jewish people, who had already suffered so much.

"You look nothing *like* Anne," the drama teacher had said gently as Debra sobbed in his office for all the injustice in the world the day the cast list went up.

"But! I'm! *Jewish!* She could have been *me!*" First a brilliant and beautiful young girl killed by Nazis, now this. It was more than Debra could bear. She had been cast as the understudy for Miep.

The woman in the muumuu seems to be waiting for Debra to either muster up some Portuguese or go away.

"Services?" Debra says, waiting for that moment when it becomes clear to the woman that she should envelop Debra in some sort of embrace. "Shabbat?" She fingers the phrase book but knows that nothing in it will be of any help. It is broken down into five sections: Conversation, Food, Transportation, Hospitality, Emergencies. There are things she wants to communicate that are not included in these basics. Were there a Religion-Seeking section, perhaps things would be easier. "I have come for Shabbat services," Debra would say. "I am a Jew." And then, ritually, defensively, to explain her visage: "My mother converted." Then she would flip over to the Food section: "What's for dinner?"

The woman crosses her arms over her chest. They face off in monolingual obtuseness.

Okay, Debra thinks. It is Friday night; there must be Shabbat services. There are certain immutable rules involved with religion. Just because she is in a borderline second-world country (bastard child of Europe)—a place where she had, the day before, for complete lack of alternative cuisine, been forced to eat *tripe,* for fuck's sake—does not mean that she should feel stupid for having shown up, unannounced, at Lisbon's only synagogue, sans a way back, at dusk on Shabbat. A Jew could do that, find a home anywhere in the world with other Jews. Wasn't that the point of the entire freakin' deal? Covenant, whatever? There'd been a song at camp one summer, when Debra was old enough for irony but not too old to sing songs: "Wherever you go, there's always someone Jewish/you're never alone when you say you're a Jew/so when you're not home and you're somewhere kind of newish/the odds are, don't look far, 'cause they're Jewish, too!"

"Services? *La servisa? Unas servesas?*" Oh, this is pathetic. Debra has taken rudimentary Spanish and knows that *cerveza* is the word for beer.

The woman wags an index finger in Debra's face. "No," she grunts, clipped and guttural. She turns and walks back into the synagogue.

Debra had envisioned ecstatic hora dancing, tears of welcoming and joy, universal language, belonging. *Oh,* they'd say, *a fellow Jew, here to observe the Sabbath with us; we are but one family tree, with branches spread over the world!* She'd envisioned laughing in the face of genocide, expulsion, Cindy Torricelli. She'd envisioned *Shabbat shalom,* simple language she could share without embarrassment or desperate phrase book searching. Anything to counterbalance the past three weeks of backpacking alone: a latter-day version, with a state-of-the-art backpack, of the Wandering Jew.

Debra sits down on the sidewalk, places her flip-flopped

feet in an ever-shrinking patch of sunlight to warm them, and waits.

She was supposed to have stayed in Spain for a few days before going on to France, but she'd left after a single miserable night at the Marbella youth hostel. "Nice to meet you," she'd said to a pair of tall German girls in her dorm room, thinking, "What were your grandparents doing during the war?" The hostel contingent congregated at Joe's Garage, a bar owned by an American ex-pat, where only English was spoken and back-packers imbibed to the thumping bass of the Violent Femmes and U2. This was not what Debra had come for. She wanted windswept beaches, charming towns bordered by overgrown fields, singular cafés in which she could write passionately about self-sufficiency in her journal and strike up conversations with ruggedly handsome, multilingual local tradesmen. She wandered the streets in disgust. Sunburned British families enraptured by Andeans in matching woven ponchos playing ABBA songs on panpipes, Spanish runaways at folding tables hawking temporary tattoos, the yellow-and-red glow of a gigantic McDonald's casting everyone in a nightmarish light. Debra had felt claustrophobic and totally, invertedly foreign. She'd conducted a brief, informal poll of some of her fellow hostelers the next morning and found that not one of them had included Portugal on their itineraries.

The woman reappears through the gate with a small, be-spectacled man in tow. She speaks to him in rapid-fire Portuguese, gesturing toward Debra.

"Hello," the man says to Debra, holding out a flaccid, dry hand. "I'm Sergio. Can I help you?" His English is perfect; he's been educated. A person of the book.

"We're the people of the book," Debra's mother often says, embracing her chosen religion like a dyed-in-the-wool zealot. "We Jews, we study wherever in the world we are, we know that learning is a priority, we understand the importance of *knowledge*." Debra never has the heart to interrupt and clarify that the "book" to which that colloquialism refers is actually the *Bible,* not Every Book Ever Written. Her mother was such a smug convert, such an emphatic user of the first person plural. "*We* are the *chosen* people." Chosen, chosen, chosen. Her mother had chosen to be chosen, and so theirs was a revival house; a twenty-four-hour religious pep rally designed to legitimize them both. Because Judaism, like baldness, is matrilineal.

Debra smiles at Sergio, pumps his limp hand. "I was hoping to come to Shabbat services," she says. She is paranoid and assumes there is a problem, if not with her *shiksa* face, then with her shoes (Americans! Coming to shul in *sandals!* The nerve!). It was a toss-up between the hiking boots and the flip-flops; she'd had to make a choice. She'd jokingly, inappropriately pretended, sitting on her thin, musty mattress at the *pensão,* that she was an alternate version of Styron's Sophie: Choose one pair of shoes! Choose, or you lose them both! In a mock panic, acting out the Oscar clip, she'd gone with the flip-flops.

Sergio smiles as if he feels very, very sorry for her and blinks his bulging wet marble eyes. Debra instinctively braces herself for it: *My, you certainly don't look Jewish.*

"I'm afraid that the synagogue is closed. We are open as a museum Monday to Friday, from ten a.m. to six p.m."

She'd been lying in her postcards ("an amazing museum, full

of painted tiles called *azulejos!*), embarrassed to admit that she had not been inside one museum in two weeks of travel (*so* not WALGWD!), preferring instead to while away the hours shopping at markets or at cafés, reading.

"But it's Shabbat," Debra says, torn between relief (that there is no issue with either her footwear or face) and incomprehension (that there could indeed be a synagogue where Shabbat goes unheralded). Her voice is plaintive, whiny, keening: embarrassingly revealing of her deepest needs and impossible to accept as her own. She wonders for a brief, flickering moment if perhaps this is in fact a sort of *Marrano* protocol—if these people might automatically deny active practice of Judaism for the sake of their own sense of safety and well-being. If, somewhere beneath the synagogue "museum," there might still be a system of tunnels opening up into a dank cave where women in lace head coverings thrice waved their hands over freshly lit candles and sang the blessing together. If only she knew the secret code! Could she wink a few times? Slip him a twenty, tell him *Al* sent her, give him a choreographed handshake?

"There are not enough Jews left here for a minyan," Sergio says. "Not for a long time. There are only about eighty of us in total, and most are not observant at all."

"Oh," says Debra, glancing around at the neighboring houses. Quickly, so he can dismiss it as a tic if he so chooses, she catches Sergio's eye and blinks twice, theatrically. *I'm one of you, let me in.*

"Many tourists come here," he says. "It is a shame, because the tourists probably could help for a minyan." He shakes his head and paraphrases for Ms. Muumuu, who rolls her eyes

35

and walks back into the building without another look at Debra. "You'll come back on Monday, yes? I hope?"

The sun has almost completely disappeared now, and Shabbat has officially begun. Fuck this, Debra thinks. She has come all this way, over oceans, through tourist traps, bearing her aloneness righteously, and the Jews of Lisbon have let her down by allowing themselves to disappear into thin air, like spots you see when you stand up too quickly. She will not, as she hoped, be welcomed into the bosom of a familiar language-and-culture-gap-defying entity. She can scream it from rooftops: *I'm a Jew!* But here is another way in which it does not amount to crap, does not entitle her to anything tangible.

So, okay, screw it. Instead she will go back to her *pensão*, she will put on some lip gloss, she will go to a club in the Barrio Alto and listen to *fado* and drink port and let some Italian tourist hit on her. This will be her own personal Shabbat observance. She will go where her phrase book can help her. She will pick up her literal and proverbial backpack and move on.

"Are you here alone?" Sergio smiles benevolently at her. He checks his watch. Looks around at the empty, silent street.

Debra winces at this question, hates that he will not understand why a nice young girl would travel all by herself, that he will pity her the way her parents do. "Don't you want to go with some friends or something, honey?"

"Yes," she says, affecting hardness for his sake and her own. She continues, defensively, the same way she might admit to a roomful of Sisterhood ladies that her mother converted. "Lots of American women travel by themselves. It's perfectly normal." Of course she would rather have gone traveling with some friends. But her friends were starting grad school, or working eighty-hour weeks at new investment-banking jobs, or broke.

"Yes," he says. "Of course. You are staying in Lisbon?"

"Yeah." Debra wants to use the phone to call a cab or something, but she knows that use of the phone is prohibited on Shabbat. So she'll have to turn her back on the synagogue-cum-museum, which remains dark inside even though the sun is gone, and walk to one of the houses. "But don't worry, I have a cab coming back for me. I'm just going to go wait on the sidewalk."

It's the old counterprerejection ploy, so useful in her dealings with various ambivalent boys and men over the years: Once the whiff of rebuff is in the air, act fast and make it all seem like your idea. No thank you, vanished secret Jews and ritual-laden converts of Lisbon; I have many better things to do than pay my respects to the last vestiges of your existence! No thank-you, drama department of Taft Junior High, I think I will join the madrigal society! Really, Tom, Dick, Ezra—I am not ready for a serious relationship quite yet!

"Okay, then." Sergio holds out his dead-animal hand and heads around the back of the building. "*Shabbat shalom,*" he says over his shoulder, an afterthought. It's sweet, the way he says it: soaked in nostalgia, trying it on for size.

"*Obrigada,*" Debra says, even though it has a thick, unwieldy feel coming out of her mouth in speaking to someone who knows her entire language; makes her feel like a fraud for attempting the proper pronunciation of this one paltry word.

She walks up to the door of a house across the street and

opens her phrase book to the Emergencies section, where she finds the words for "I need to use your telephone" before ringing the bell. Nothing is at stake here; unspoken international human kindness dictates that she will be allowed to use a phone, will be helped safely back to her *pensão,* will continue to write postcards and amass ticket stubs, will go home and make a scrapbook. But perhaps, in molding this story into an anecdote, Debra will modify it so that the woman who answers the door appears at first to have a fantastical halo of light around her head, which, after a beat, Debra sees is just the overhead light in the entry hall of the house. Perhaps she will say that she could see from the door two candles in old silver candlesticks, burning in the window.

"Entrar!" the woman will say with a smile in Debra's retelling: "Come in."

So Long

My best friend, Rachel, now insists she be called Ra-chel. "Ra" as in the sun god, "chel" as in "hell" pronounced by someone drowning in their own phlegm. Emphasis on the "chel." She's been born again.

"My Jewish *neshama* was in hiding all this time," explains Ra-chel, who's wearing an ankle-length skirt and long-sleeved shirt even though it's mid-August, almost ninety degrees out and humid. We're sitting in a salon, waiting for her hairstylist to come and fetch us.

"What the fuck is a *neshama*?" I ask.

"It's the essence of your soul," she says. This from the girl who, in the ninth grade, using a peeled cucumber, taught me how to give a proper blow job.

"Oh," I say.

We're here to cut off all her hair. Specifically we're here to cut off all her hair so that she can cover her head with a wig made out of someone else's hair. It's like a bad *Twilight Zone*.

On the plus side of having your best friend get swept up into religious extremity are the following: nonmodest wardrobe inheritance ("It's not *tzniut*," Ra-chel says, holding her favorite black tank top out to me. "What the fuck is *tzniut?*" I say, taking it happily) and the runoff of all her new-found information ("Modesty," she says. "Women's bodies are sacred"). This from the girl who, in the tenth grade, flashed a tit at the hot math teacher and got suspended.

She's getting married in a few days.

"*Mazel tov*," I said brightly when she told me the news. Limited as my knowledge of Judaism might be, I knew, at least, that "*Mazel tov*" is what you say in such situations. I grew up way more observant than our sweet born-again. She didn't even have a bat mitzvah. At mine she skipped out on the Torah service to sneak a cigarette with Ethan Zacharias in the parking lot. So you'll forgive me if this zero-to-sixty re-ligiosity of hers is a bit hard to swallow (so to speak—we're talking about a girl who, in the eleventh grade, told a depart-ment store makeup lady that semen was the secret to her lu-minous complexion).

Her intended's name is Dov. He's *ba'al tshuva,* like her. It means "returned." (Don't kid yourself: born again). There's, like, a whole world of these people. You wouldn't know it, they don't tend to host telethons or anything, but they're out there. Dov used to be *Doug,* for fuck's sake. He's from San Diego.

"Rach, you're twenty-four," I told her.

"So?" she said.

"So you're too young to get married," I said. Dov is thirty-one. He has a beard. He used to be a professional surfer.

They met two years ago at Burning Man and bonded over Phish bootlegs.

"Miri," she said. "Try and be happy for me."

"I am," I said, meaning I was trying. "I *am* happy for you."

I'm to be Ra-chel's maid of honor. I still have the half-a-heart charm split with her when we were nine that proclaims us "Best Friends 4ever!" (my half says "ends" and "ver!"). But even so the bride-to-be has new friends. Chava, Leora, Batya. Rachel met them on a religious weekend retreat with Doug/Dov, on her way to becoming Ra-chel.

It's a week before doomsday, and we're all sitting in a booth at a theme bar. The theme is a little muddled, but seems to have something to do with the tropics. This is made clear by the papier-mâché palm trees strung with lights and the waitresses in grass skirts and coconut shell bras.

The girls are drinking kosher champagne, which they smuggled in here themselves; I'm doing shots. Ra-chel is sporting a ridiculous tuft of white lace, meant to approximate a veil, tucked, via a comb, into the crown of her head.

I hold up a Black and Gold. *"L'chaim,"* I say, trying and failing not to sound sarcastic. When I toss it back, Chava and Leora exchange looks and Batya *ptu-ptu-ptu*s over her shoulder. These women know how to party.

This is my first ever bachelorette celebration, but to the best of my knowledge, they're supposed to consist of drunken frolicking, the sort ostensibly verboten after marriage, aren't they? Hairless, body-glittered men gyrating in your face, that sort of thing? So it's something of a disappointment to be sitting here instead, watching Chava trying not to stare at the shell-titted waitresses, discussing the head covering Ra-chel will have to don as a married lady. Hat, cloth, or wig? These are her options. After she's married, only Dov is supposed to see her hair.

Batya is holding forth on wigs made from human hair. "They're beautiful," she says dreamily. "My cousin Malka got one from France. It cost like two thousand dollars." As an unmarried woman, Batya herself is still allowed to walk around uncovered. Hair, see, is erotic. Unmodest. Not *tzniut.*

"So you can cover your own hair with someone *else's,* and that's okay?" I ask. "That makes zero sense." The axis of observance glares at me.

"It's a loophole, sorta," Ra-chel tells me apologetically. How on earth can she buy into this shit? Here she sits, daintily sipping her kosher champagne, the girl who was hospitalized freshman year of college after doing her own weight in Jell-o shots at a frat party.

"Well, it's pretty fucking dumb."

We sit in silence for a moment, shaking our heads, defining ourselves by what we're not, the simplest thing to do. So definitive, so satisfying.

Batya changes the subject. "How's the dress?"

Christ, the dress is huge. A real puff pastry. Up to her neck, down to the floor, hugging both wrists. Very modest indeed. Not quite what I'd pictured for her when we went through our *Bride's* magazine phase the summer after sixth grade. I down another shot, dramatically tossing my head back and slamming the glass onto the table when I've emptied it.

"Good," says Ra-chel. "Had my last fitting yesterday." She winks at me, conciliatory. We'd spent the day together. First lunch at a kosher restaurant, then the fitting, then a mati-nee. I'd almost forgotten all about her transformation and im-pending marital imprisonment, I was so happy to be alone with her in that secular milieu. Though it was kind of un-comfortable when the movie, a supernatural romantic com-edy, turned out to have a lot of sex in it. Rachel, back when she was still Rachel, was quite the whore. And I mean that as a compliment. Anyway, I kept glancing over at her out of the corner of my eye, wondering if it made her uncomfort-able now, to have done all the stuff she did. And I would have asked her about it, but shit: There's this opaque cur-tain that seems to have gone up between us, this unspeak-able chasm between me and her, and I'm not at all entitled to her like I used to be.

The shots, meanwhile, are taking full effect. "Is this the lit-tle girl I carried?" I sling an arm around Ra-chel's shoulder and force her to sway with me as I sing. "Is this the little girl at play?" She hates it when I reference *Fiddler on the Roof,* but honestly, it's the closest I can get these days to understanding what the fuck is happening with her.

"Miri," she says, wriggling out from under my arm and gig-gling despite herself, despite the curtain, then rolling her eyes for the benefit of the girls. But I'm still thinking about the wig thing, about Ra-chel covering up Rachel's famous, gorgeous mane.

"Are you really going to wear a wig?" I ask softly.

"Miri." She says my name with pity in her voice, like I'm so in the dark, so far behind. "My hair is only for my husband to see." This stings, somehow. Another kind of club of which I am not a member.

"The thing is, okay, if your hair is so, like, *dangerously* enticing to the world, what's different about a human hair wig that probably looks *better* than your own hair?" This must hit its mark with Leora, especially, whose scalp is visible beneath the lankest, mousiest excuse for a head of hair I've ever seen. "Hair that looks *better* than your own would be, like, even *more* erotic." Do I imagine the girls squirming at the *e* word? Do I want them to squirm? I give my own hair a toss, feeling it fall across my neck, against the side of my face. I make bedroom eyes at Batya.

Somewhere above our heads, a vision of myself—in knee-highs and a red cape—dives down: avenger of religious absolutism. If only I could scoop Ra-chel up into my arms and carry her off into the parallel universe in which she is still Rachel, good old Rachel, where she would never in a million years wear a motherfucking *wig,* where we link arms and fly together through our postadolescence an unchanged unit, hair billowing behind us in the wind.

"I mean, have you guys thought about whose hair it is, anyhow?" The girls stare at the point where the wall and ceiling meet. "Fucking destitute cancer patients—"

"Miri," says Ra-chel. "Come on." She's fairly used to my bullshit at this point and very magnanimously lets it roll off her back most of the time. Any day now I fully expect her to 86 me anyhow. My name is beginning to sound like a disease when she says it.

"Sorr-y," I say, only slightly less sincere an offering than my *Mazel tov* or *L'chaim.* "It's just weird."

"You should try to be more respectful," Batya tells me, chest all puffed out. I guess I missed the *Wild Kingdom* that illuminated fighting techniques of the Urban Fervently Religious.

"Go take a ritual bath," I mutter, consumed with the effort it's taking me not to cry.

"You act like you're not Jewish," says Chava. "It's not some weird cult, you know." Is there anything more condescending than being pitied for not having seen the light?

"Perhaps I should come along to a weekend retreat, hmmm? Learn a bit about my faith?" I realize as I say it that I am a child of divorce with one, two, three, *four* empty shot glasses in front of me: a perfect candidate for rebirth. Goddammit, I hate when sarcasm bites itself in the ass. The thought silences me for a few seconds, and the triumvirate makes an instantaneous, unanimous decision to ignore me. They act this out by conversing among themselves in Hebrew, which, though I made it through six (count 'em, like rings around the stump of my psyche!) years in Sunday school, I can't remotely understand.

"Hey," I say. "Hey, you guys." They look at me. "Have you guys heard about Weird Al Yankovic?" Blank stares all around. "You know, Weird Al? Weird Al! Remember him?"

"Yeah," Batya says, finally, grudgingly. I feel triumphant for some reason, elated to have evidence that we all come from the same place: watching television in our pajamas in the early eighties. "What about him?"

"Yeah," I say. "So Weird Al has been kind of off the radar for a while now, hasn't he?" They don't trust me. "He has! He has! So, you know *why* he's been off the radar lately?" Nothing. "Seriously, do you know *why*?"

45

"No, Miri," Batya says finally, deadpan. "Why has Weird Al been off the radar?"

"Because." I pause. "Because . . ." I give them the old eyeball sweep. "Drumroll . . . He's *ba'al tshuva*! I'm serious! He lives in the West Bank and he's got like eight kids and he studies Torah all day long!" I turn to Ra-chel. "I've been meaning to tell you that." The truth is I have no idea why Weird Al's career is in the toilet. This just struck me suddenly as a totally believable and timely urban legend to start.

"Is that true?" Chava asks the others. They shrug but look intrigued.

I grab a massively shell-titted waitress passing by. "What can I have that's nice and fruity and frothy and girly?" This is, lest we forget, a bachelorette party.

She thinks hard for a moment. "A Cool Breeze . . . ?"

I make eye contact with Batya and pretend to contemplate deeply before turning back to the waitress. "Does it have pork in it?"

"Um, I don't think so," she says, looking around for someone with seniority.

"Fabulous," I say. "Bring me one of those!"

The woman of the hour, meanwhile, looks miserable. I offer a small smile, fluff her veil. Her hair is long, thick, and bouncy as a shampoo commercial. She used to do disgusting things to it: mayonnaise, beer, raw eggs. And suddenly I can see what they mean about modesty or whatever, because I can hardly stand the sight of her familiar, beseeching face framed by that proliferate hair.

I grab her by the shoulders and lay a hard, loud smooch against her cheek.

She rolls her eyes and giggles. "You're wasted."

I forget for a second that I am, in fact, intoxicated, and take her statement to mean: I am a wasted soul, a free-floating *ne-shama,* an areligious husk of no use to my people.

"Yup." I am, I suppose, wasted. I stand up slowly when the waitress comes back with my drink. "Where is the restroom, *por favor?*" She points to the back corner of the room and I curtsy, offer the girls a salute.

The room is fluid as I make my way toward the Ladies, like walking on a waterbed. Seedlings turn overnight to sunflow-ers, something something something.

Peeing is cathartic, a relief, and when I'm done I feel calmed, heightened, a clarity of consciousness that comes close to revelation but doesn't quite touch it. A-*ha!* Urination-as-religion. I sit directly on the toilet seat (a confirmation, if one was lacking, of my inebriation), relishing my empty blad-der, the disgusting bar bathroom smells, the graffiti on the walls. Some people have these feelings of utter aliveness when they've reached the summit of a mountain, given birth, found religion, but they've got nothing on the first, overdue pee of a long, alcohol-fueled evening. I consider this as I pe-ruse the chaos of "Ally is an a-hole," "I like cocks," "Eat me," "Love is the answer!" Close to the back wall is one in small capital letters, in a straight, un-bar-bathroom-like line: NO JESUS, NO PEACE, KNOW JESUS, KNOW PEACE. How would it feel to embrace this statement wholly? Could I walk back out into the bar a believer?

I try and I try, but the longer I stare at the words, willing them to make some sort of a dent, the less sense they make. After a while the lines and curves of the letters look completely foreign, and there's some chick banging on the door, asking did I fall in.

I linger, though, thinking about the time in elementary school when Rachel conspired to have me catch her chicken pox so we could stay home, watching TV and lounging in oatmeal baths together. She breathed in my face, licked my utensils, pressed her red-flecked arms against me, kissed me on the lips. But it didn't work; I turned out to be immune or something and had to go to school without her for a week that felt like a month.

In the salon, I decide to take a new tack, reframe things: this is like some sort of a reality makeover show, and we're its stars. I intone voice-over in my head: *Watch Rachel Hassek become Ra-chel! Watch her prepare for a new life in which she fulfills the Covenant and learns to be true to her heritage!* This is all postmodern fun and games, damn it. *God* damn it. When we're done playing out this nutty scenario we'll go back to being ourselves.

"Rachel?" A guy with a nipple ring poking through his black mesh muscle tee.

"Ra-chel," she says to him, nodding, before standing up. He could give a shit about her newfound pronunciation, but I figure she's got to be insistent for her own sake. When you adopt a radical identity change, it's not just other people you have to remind, right? I gather up our bags and a few magazines from the rack and we follow him through the salon to the last in a row of swivel chairs in front of backlit mirrors.

"Nikki will be with you shortly." The guy pivots theatrically and walks away.

Rachel-cum-Ra-chel plops down into the chair and begins to swivel to and fro. I look through my pile of magazines. A *Glamour*, a *Vanity Fair*, and a super cheesy salon-trade magazine called *Hairdooz*.

"Thanks for coming with," she says, her voice small under the dull roar of hairdryers and techno. I'm really, really trying to go with the flow here.

"Sure."

"It means a lot to me that you're supporting me," she says. This is kind of like she's talking to a six-year-old. Using persuasive preemption while the kid holds a scissors and eyes the dog: *I'm so glad you're not going to use that scissors to cut off the dog's tail!* I myself am quite familiar with this tack, having spent like the entire twelfth grade baby-sitting.

I grin at her. "Want me to do mine in solidarity?"

She's looking at herself in the mirror, trying, if I had to guess, to memorize the sight of herself in this soon-to-be former incarnation.

"Remember when we were little," she says dreamily, "and we used to look at ourselves in my mom's bathroom mirror? The one with the row of lights on the top?"

I nod. "Dorks." Mrs. Hassek would let us play with her makeup and jewelry, and we'd do ourselves up, as only drag queens and little girls can, in feathers and pearls, bright red lips and cheeks, aquamarine eyelids, penciled-on beauty marks.

"Yeah," she says, staring into space. She turns back toward the mirror. "I used to squint at myself and, like, blur my vi-

49

sion? So I couldn't really see myself? And I thought if I squinted hard enough I would be able to see what I would look like when I grew up."

"And?" I remember thinking twenty was about as old as I'd ever get. And I guess I sort of still feel that way. Which is to say that now I'm all of twenty-four and I have no idea what happens from here on in.

"And what?"

"Do you look like you thought you'd look?"

She snaps out of it, sighs. "Dude," she says, "I was being philosophical."

"Dude," I say, emphasis on the first part of the one syllable.

"Dude," she repeats, emphasis on the middle. This is our way of communicating without real words, borne of many an afternoon spent together in a stoned haze, giggling at everything, nothing, whatever.

"Oh, hey. I almost forgot!" I open up my bag and produce a small gold box, tied ornately with red-and-gold ribbon, which contains a single Godiva truffle. Fucking eight bucks. "I thought this would be appropriate," I tell her. It's a sincere wish (Yes! Sincere! Fuck off!) that her life with Dov (and with God, I suppose) be a sweet one. And also a nod to her soon-to-be-disposed-of hair.

She grins, takes it from my outstretched hand. "Thanks." Then she turns it over and scours the box for assurance that it's Kosher.

I open up *Hairdooz* to find that it's comprised of full-color head shots of women with extreme hairstyles, each accompanied by a horrible pun. "Oh my God—this is priceless! Rachel, look at this."

She narrows her eyes at me, curls her lip, adopts a singsong tone. "Let's play a game. Can you tell me which two words in your last statement were problematic?"

She has a thing about taking God's name in vain. And *Rachel,* crap.

"*My* God doesn't mind if you invoke His presence at the scene of such high kitsch," I tell her, holding up the first page of *Hairdooz,* where a picture of a woman with unnaturally straight hair is attended by the caption "Ironed Maiden."

"You have a relationship with God!" she squeals. "*Baruch Hashem.*"

That must mean something along the lines of "Hallelujah," because she says it whenever things go well for her. We made the two o'clock show—*Baruch Hashem!* The light seems to be turning green for us—*Baruch Hashem!* Dov and I are getting married—*Baruch Hashem!*

"'Beyond the Fringe,'" I read, turning the page to a picture of a woman with thick bangs covering her eyes. "Like you."

Nikki, our stylist, materializes from behind a curtain and dives right in, massaging Ra-chel's scalp with her fingers. "Hey, baby. God, look at this gorgeous hair. What are we doing to it?"

"We're takin' it *allll* off," says Ra-chel, affecting nonchalance. The last time I heard her string those words together, she was referring to her masterminded plot to streak Homecoming sophomore year of high school.

I hold *Hairdooz* up for Nikki. "Cream of the Cropped," I tell her, pointing to the image, a modified bowl cut.

"*Really?*" says Nikki, horrified that Ra-chel would do away with so much healthy, beautiful hair.

"Don't ask," I say, turning the page to a picture of a woman with sharply angled layers. "Be Blunt," it said, like live commentary. Although it might be fun, I reconsider, to hear Rachel try to explain the concept of modesty, taken to the nth degree, to Nikki, who is wearing a micromini and navel-baring tank top.

Rachel just nods, looking equal parts determined and terrified.

"Wow! 'Kay. Customer's always right. Let's get you washed." Nikki leads her to the row of sinks and helps her into position while I flip pages with increasingly lame captions like "What About Bob?" and "Wanna Shag?"

There was this one Halloween, circa tenth grade or so, when neighborhood guys thought it would be hilarious to smear the girls with Nair instead of the usual shaving cream. I was Carrie that year, wearing the requisite prom dress, tiara, and long blond wig, all of which I had found at a thrift store and doused thoroughly with strawberry syrup. Rachel was Robert Smith from the Cure. She teased her dark hair into a spiky inviolate mass and powdered her face all white and found black lipstick at CVS. We crushed and snorted some of her little brother's Ritalin, which, in combination with the couple of beers my dad didn't notice taken from the fridge, put us in a nice state. Neither of us remembers much of the evening, but when it was over, Rachel had a giant bald spot on the left side of her head, where someone had gotten her with the Nair, which, of course, we had assumed was simply shaving cream. I, with my Carrie wig, had been protected.

You would have thought she'd been gang-raped, she was so inconsolable about that bald spot. Which I admit looked freaky and pretty terrible, but still. The pitch and intensity of her tears, the weeping over that patch of missing hair, the cursing out of the "provincial motherfucking assholes" who had nothing better to do than this kind of "infantile desecration"—it was horrible. I hugged her and promised her over and over again that it would grow back, it would grow back, it would grow back, but she just kept wailing, "When?" "When?"

When Ra-chel returns, her hair is dripping and she looks small, as though seen from a great distance. I watch her closely, trying to tune out the echoes of her fifteen-year-old voice, begging me to tell her *when* her hair would grow back. *When?*

"You know what I'm thinking?" she asks me as Nikki snaps a monster-size bib around her neck and begins to comb out her hair.

"No," I say. Most often now I have no fucking clue whatsoever what she's thinking. "What are you thinkng?"

"I want to say the *Shehechiyanu*," she says. "Will you say it with me?"

"Explain," I say. In my lap *Hairdooz* is open to a picture of a woman who looks like she's put her finger in a socket and died wearing her huge frozen smile and stair-step curls. I keep my hand over the caption and challenge myself to come up with a good one, but give up characteristically quickly and look at the one printed: "Crimp in Your Style."

"It's the blessing of firsts, I guess," she says. "For special moments. When you feel the miracle of life and are grateful for having reached this day." Clearly she's been coached in the answer to that one.

"Oh," I say. I am trying to be happy for her, I am trying to be happy for her, I am trying to be happy for her. But do I want only her happiness? Or do I want her to stay as she was, as she's always been, with me? And if she isn't un-changed, if she's no longer mine, do I care about her happi-ness at all?

"I just want to be true to my heritage," she told me when she got back from that first, influential retreat. "I just want to find out what it means to be Jewish. I just want to live my life to its fullest potential."

"Cool," I'd said. "But why can't you just go take a Land-mark Forum life-skills seminar like everybody else?"

Now I smile broadly at her. That I sit here and hold her hand and say nothing while she blesses her choices is not too much to ask, is it? No, it is not. I'm a fucking bitch, is the truth. "Bring it."

She reaches over for my hand, and I catch Nikki averting her gaze. *"Baruch ata Adonai,"* Ra-chel begins, and that part I recognize from my family's once-a-year visits to temple, but the rest is fuzzy and fast and doesn't really register. At the end she opens her eyes and squeezes my hand.

"Amen," I say, using up what feels like the last of my breath, hoping I don't invalidate her prayer, cancel her out.

Nikki has finished combing out Ra-chel's hair and is bran-dishing a shiny pair of scissors. "You sure about this?"

It's that speak-now-or-forever-hold-your-peace moment, but I let it pass, looking at Rachel's reflection in the mirror, committing her to memory.

Then, amid all the other shedding and casting off and walk-ing away redone, Nikki holds out a ponytail of Ra-chel's hair, opens gaping scissors around it maybe four or five inches from her head, and works them closed like a gnawing animal.

The big clump of hair flops to the ground around our feet, and I gather it into a plastic bag for some unlucky kid with cancer. Then Nikki begins to snip away, with a smaller scissors now, fashioning a cute shag that will never see the light of day. I continue looking through *Hairdooz,* Nero fiddling, with an insouciance I have to work hard to maintain. On the last page is one that makes my heart skitter: a picture of a faceless woman with extraordinarily long hair. It falls like water past her shoulders, down her arched back, past her waist and out of the frame. "So Long!" it says blithely. Never say good-bye, I've heard; good-bye is final. Say "So long" instead, and hope to meet again.

I hold the magazine up so Rachel-cum-Ra-chel can see it, a complete and not entirely unhappy farewell. "'So Long!'" I say, pointing, but she's not paying attention to me. She's looking at herself in the mirror, transfixed, taking in her strange, shocking lack of hair. This is the most irrevocable of her many changes. She could grow it all back if she wanted to, but it would take a long time.

Everything But

On their way to temple, Alex will not shut up. "My Torah portion was *Toldot*," he says. It's 10:30. They're late. "Jacob and Esau."

In the back Gertie is strapped into her car seat and is staring, brow knit, out the window. Erin checks her watch. Services started at 9:45.

"Is Dorit going whole hog with this? Like, actually reading from the Torah?" Dorit, bat mitzvah girl, is Alex's niece, daughter of his only sister, Dana. Alex ignores the question, tinged as it is with Erin's well-worn superiority and sarcasm: an overt comment on poor Dorit's intelligence and general worth, a covert attack on her doltish mother, Alex's beloved big sister. Dana. Alex looks at his watch.

"We're late," he sighs.

"No shit."

They're late because Gertie had refused to be dressed in her temple outfit, an itchy green velvet number with matching barrettes. The green ensemble had mysteriously brought forth dramatic screeches of protest and vehement, back-and-forth head whips. Gertie had ducked out of reach, shrank from the dress like a soul from the light.

"They grow up so quickly, don't they?" Erin said when finally they'd managed to wrangle her into the car at 10:15 after plying her with bribes and promises of future bribes, late, late, late. Alex blames Erin for these mishaps. As a mother, little things throw her completely. More than a year and a half in, even, she feels wholly unprepared for and amateurish at it, embarrassed that something like a temper tantrum over a dress could so derail them from the course of their daily lives. It wasn't normal to be forty-five minutes late because your toddler had refused to acquiesce to your choice of outfit for her, was it? Or did most people simply wrench their child into the dress, throw their child into the car, and show up only slightly harried at, say, 10:00?

"Jacob and Esau," Alex keeps saying, over and over, like a rap, absentmindedly drumming his thumbs on the steering wheel as he waits to turn left at a green light. He inches forward into the intersection, thumb-drumming in time with the *click-clack!* of the left turn signal. He glances at Gertie in the rearview to see if she's up for a sing-along. Erin watches him, irritated that he doesn't seem to care that she's watching him, does not turn to look at her, does not acknowledge her gaze. It makes her want to dig her nails into his eye sockets, rake them down his face with all the force she can muster, hold his eyes open like in a torture chamber or laser eye surgery, make him Look At Her. She's heard about his bar mitzvah a hundred times, heard him laugh exclusively at his own memories of the kid he'd been. Some girl had given him head in the bathroom at the synagogue during his party. "I became a man that day," he'd say, guffawing (yes, truly: guffawing), rolling his eyes for the benefit of anyone who'd heard the story before (Erin had!); he was a narcissistic motherfucker, but it would be terrible to appear *unselfconsciously* so. This Erin had mistaken for acute self-awareness and good humor when they'd first met and for way (*way!*) too long afterward.

"I have no idea what mine was," Erin tells him, though he didn't ask and most certainly wasn't going to. At Erin's bat mitzvah her mother had been fighting the first of three rounds with cancer ("female trouble," she had called it, with rueful cheer) and wore a terrible, off-color wig. In all the pictures Sheila and Erin both look like sideshow wax dummies of themselves: Erin at thirteen with acne and temporarily lop-sided features; Sheila with her reproductive organs newly evacuated and that slick greenish-white chemo sheen, which was only exacerbated by the orange tint to what was sup-posed to have been a brunette wig. The photos themselves were practically radioactive with indignity and ugliness. Erin had hauled out the albums in Phoenix after the funeral: Noth-ing like a funeral for nostalgia and fucking. Though of course there'd been no fucking; Alex had barely touched her since even before Gertie, and acted all put out and harassed when-ever she tried to initiate. A big letdown after *shiva* each night, truth be told. It had occurred to Erin, immediately after the eulogies and kaddish and burial and *Yes, thank you, I know, Me toos,* that this terrible thing, the loss of her mom, might ac-tually, finally, get her laid. But no.

"Jacob and Esau," Alex says again, and now Erin is intent on recalling her own bat mitzvah *parsha.* Those heinous posed pictures are clear as crystal (her older brother, Jonathan, with his feathered eighties mullet and lingering baby fat, her younger sister, Julie, in a sea green puffy dress with shoulder pads), but the real issue of the day, the Torah portion she'd memorized phonetically with the help of a then-state-of-the-art Walkman and on which she'd composed a two-page single-spaced speech, is nowhere to be found.

"Jesus," she says, squinting. "What the fuck was mine?"

Alex looks toward her sharply. "Hey," he says. He juts his head toward the backseat, where Gertie sits, miserable and impervious, in her green dress. They have a deal about swearing in front of Gertie. A convoluted system of perfunctory favors and chores invented when Gertie had first started talking and had echoed some perverse one-off.

Erin rubs her forehead, squeezes her eyes shut, skipping stones on the lake of memory. The brown industrial carpeting of the synagogue, her first manicure (a beige-pink called "Poundcake"), a run in those horribly elastic flesh-colored panty hose, noticed only after she'd chanted the *haftorah*.

"Why can't I remember what my stupid fucking *parsha* was?"

Alex offers a shadow of a shrug, thumbs-drumming in time with, Erin imagines, his self-satisfied internal repetition of *Jacob and Esau, Jacob and Esau, Jacob and Esau.*

It's 10:32 and they're still sitting in the middle of the intersection a few blocks from the synagogue, waiting to turn left. The light turns yellow, finally, and an advancing truck seems unsure whether or not to go for it. Alex assumes not and takes his foot off the brake, only to slam it back down again as the truck keeps coming at them. Then, when the truck driver slows, motions for them to go ahead, Alex, afraid that it's a limited-time-only offer, slams on the gas, hurtling them through the turn so they all get pinned to their seats with centrifugal force, like on a roller coaster. There is a small squeal of burnt rubber. Gertie lets out what from another kid might be a simple giggle, but from her is a throaty, one-note "Heh." Erin glares at him.

"Sor-ry," Alex says softly, to neither of them. He's the king of such apologies: sincere enough but directed aimlessly out into the universe, impossible to forgive.

They deposit Gertie in the nursery with the nice old lady who's been watching kids at the synagogue at least since Alex had been one. "I don't get how she's still alive," Alex always says.

"I don't get how she's still alive," Alex says. Guffaws.

The Donald and Leslie Milstein Sanctuary is gigantic and soaring, every last piece of it identified for its benefactor. Dorit, in a pink suit and matching pillbox hat, is standing on the Fred and Henrietta Beamer *bima* in between the cantor and the rabbi. Her hair is done in a lovely flip. But for her unfortunate hatchet face (a few more years and then, surely, there would be the compulsory nose job), she's Jackie O.

"Are you fucking kidding me?" Erin snorts as they settle into a pew in the back. The "fucking," she knows, is overkill. She throws it in for pure effect, for the unadulterated pleasure of it; without Gertie around she is entitled to *live,* goddammit.

"Her theme is 'Great Women from History,'" Alex informs Erin tersely, affixing a pink Nu Suede *kippah* with a bobby pin to the crown of his head. Imprinted on the underside in silver foil are the words "Bat Mitzvah of," and, in slightly bigger type, "Dorit Arad." Say something derisive about the pink *kippot,* Erin silently begs him. She opens a *siddur* to a random page and rests it in her lap. Please, she prays, say something harmlessly sardonic about the theme. What would actually be the harm in his rolling his eyes with her in tandem at this heinous display of Diaspora largesse? The *theme,* for fuck's sake!

Nadiv Arad had come to the states after serving in the Sixty-Seven War, gotten into some sort of business (no one seemed to truly have a handle on what exactly it was he did; "Property!" he would boom in his thick, charming Israeli accent when asked, but he never elaborated and was never pressed) and thereafter supplied Dana and Dorit with the biggest, least subdued home and life new money could buy, complete with eight-tone doorbell and gray marble floors throughout, two black BMWs parked around the fountain in the driveway, and the sure-to-be monstrous bat mitzvah party still to come. They're the kind of people who have no books in their house, Erin tells her friends by way of explanation. She hates them so much, and with such free-floating intensity, that she often finds herself thinking things like: It's just like them to have only had one child.

"You're a negative person," Alex spat at her when they began therapy a few months ago. To which there had been no suitable reply. *I am not* too elementary school; ditto *So what if I am?* so Erin tried to be witty and deadpan—"Go fuck yourself"—thinking the therapist would catch the irony and that Erin's sparkling, bitter wit—she was being ironic!—would thus triumph over Alex's petty self-seriousness, and they would all share a laugh. But no.

"There's your sister," Erin says acidly. Nadiv and Dana are sitting front and center in the Arnie and Mildred Pearl Pew, flanked by the grandparents. They watch Dorit a little, but mostly, instead, pursue a ravenous sanctuary stocktaking. "Hi," Dana mouths exaggeratedly at Alex, winking, kissy face. She nods slightly at Erin as her head continues on its rotating axis, eyes widening in welcome when they alight on someone else.

Dorit looks to be doing not much more than following along with the rabbi, managing to look smug and clueless at once, white *tallit* draped over narrow shoulders. Her friends, Erin can plainly see, are the Cool Kids. Boys with their hair gelled smartly, girls thin and clear-skinned, straight hair to a one, thermal reconditioning perhaps their reward for all the phonetic Hebrew memorizing. They're clustered off to one side of the chapel, so *obviously* the in-crowd, badass eighth graders who've spent this entire year of weekends at bar and bat mitzvah parties, living it up. Erin has read an article recently about even non-Jewish kids having what they'd dubbed *faux*-mitzvahs, a party, a challah, Everything But the Torah. This had been the title of the article. A mother with a name like McAdams had weighed in on her daughter's keen sense of injustice: *All her friends are having them!*

The programs, pink engraved Fabriano, are tucked into the backs of the pews, one per seat. *Welcome to My Bat Mitzvah!* Underneath her name and the date (July 30, 5765—screw the post-Christ crap) is a swirling, graceful three-dimensional ribbon (pink!) on a printed gift box. At its center is a small—the word that pops into Erin's head in the midst of this grotesqueness is actually "tasteful"—rhinestone. *This is such a special day for my family and I! Today, I am a*

Jewish adult! Today, I take on the responsibility of the Covenant! I'm so glad you could join my family and I on this very sacred day!

"What the hell was my Torah portion?" Erin whispers to Alex, increasingly frustrated by its absence from her memory. Dorit's, according to page 2, is *Vayeira*. *Vayeira is about strong women. And I wanted to honor women throughout history who are strong role models, which is fitting, since today I am a woman!*

"I don't know what the 'hell' your Torah portion was," he whispers back absently, looking at his program. "Mine was *Toldot*."

"Oh! Jacob and Esau?"

Alex turns a page unhurriedly, involves himself with Dorit's (or, more likely, Erin thinks, some hard-up and handsomely compensated rabbinical student's) explication of the superspecialty of this day. In the Cool Kids section, there is a short giggle burst followed by a prolonged *Shhhh*. Erin wishes she could go sit with them, reclaim herself at her peak. She'd been a Cool Kid, the belle of all her own bat mitzvah season's balls, her mother's simultaneous mortal illness notwithstanding. Sheila's cancer had proved, actually, quite a boon to Erin's social life. The chemo pot had been top-notch.

A Cool Kid turns around in his pew, scans the rows behind him, and locks eyes with Erin. He's a head taller than the others, looks like a delinquent, a kid held back, just about ready to procreate. The kid smiles, a smirk, no teeth exposure. Here, Erin thinks, are all the elements: the same prayer melodies, velvet-covered Torah being passed like an infant symbolically down through the generations (up on the *bima*, Alex's mother hands it over to Dana, who almost drops it before safely depositing it in Dorit's waiting, steady, pink arms), the cluster of bored pubescents yielding up one specific boy in spotlight, someone for whom to truss up later en route to the reception. So why can't she remember her *parsha*? What's in there, where this central memory might otherwise be? Her sick mother. The Thompson Twins, blaring from archaic freestanding speakers while her friends slow-danced. A beige check from her great-aunt Myrna for an unprecedented $180. An oppressed Soviet Jewish "twin"—Olga? Marianna?—denied the freedom of slow-dancing and checks, her photograph blown up and carted around like the earliest of themes, but it might as well have been a *faux*-mitzvah before its time, for the total vacuum where her Torah portion should be.

The Cool Kid—a man by now, probably, Jewishly and otherwise—turns around again, cocky and truthfully rather hot—makes Erin's head go a little dizzy. He could be my child, she thinks, and then remembers that she is, actually, someone's mother. Gertie. How completely bizarre that is. How completely fucking awful. She is in no position. Just yesterday she herself was *free,* a bat mitzvah girl, so many drugs and boys and adventures still ahead! She winks at the kid jauntily; *I'm a Cool Adult* code.

"In *my parsha,*" Dorit says, beginning the big speech, owning it with her emphasis as if Dana and Nadiv had purchased it in her honor, the Dorit Arad Torah Portion, "God reveals himself to Abraham." The program reads "G-d," like an expletive; that motherf--king a--hole. "And I've been thinking a lot about how God reveals himself all the time, and if we can even recognize him. I think sometimes we can't."

She's obviously been practicing this before the mirror for weeks, shifting the inflections, imagining her audience, relishing the profundity of it all. Erin looks down at herself, at the baby-weight belly pooch and her foreshortened thighs. At the blue veins fanning out under the thinning skin on the backsides of her hands, at her little diamond chip from Alex. "But Abraham isn't too impressed with God to offer his hospitality to strangers who come to see him. He knows that God is not more important than his fellow people. And that's something really good to remember, for all of us." *No way she did this on her own,* Erin somehow stops herself from whispering to Alex, who's beaming.

"But those strangers are *actually* God's messengers," Dorit continues. "And one of them tells Abraham's wife, Sarah, who's like a hundred years old, that she's going to have a baby in a year. But Sarah laughs in his face—Sarah laughs because she's like a hundred!" Everyone has a good chuckle at this, especially the Cool Kids. *Oh ho ho,* a fertile old lady, what a gas!

Again Erin takes a deep breath in an attempt to focus, reconnect with her memory, which she can sense is waiting, whole and hard, like a whitehead, just under the surface of the intervening years. Bat mitzvah, yes, okay; stiff Torah parchment and lilting trope, of course: yes. Braces, control top, lip gloss—check, check, check. Watered-down moral teachings extrapolated from Old Testament, yes. She concentrates hard, mental masturbation, yes, yes, yes, trying to reach the taken-for-granted orgasm right around the corner.

"Be right back," Erin says quietly to an unresponsive Alex. She waits a beat, boring imaginary holes into the side of his face, ones that ooze and hurt. Finally he turns toward her, meeting her eyes for a fraction of a second, raising his eyebrows, turning away again. *Where are you going?* He might have asked. *Are you okay?* He might've followed her out, locked them both in a bathroom stall, thrust his dick into her mouth for the first time since God knows when, giggled madly with her when they returned to the sanctuary.

She pads down the plushly carpeted aisle, out into the marble lobby and down a hallway lined with rows of high school confirmation class portraits, extending along the wall in reverse chronological order. She starts at 2003, feeling impossibly old and fat and over—her life is over! Her tits are deflated!—and proceeds, back, back, back, past the women's room door, to, ah yes, here we go, back when things made sense: '88, '87, '86 . . . Here we are: low-heeled pumps and blunt, asymmetrical haircuts; Dep and hairspray and Clearasil and Wet'n'Wild and shoulder pads and braces. And they say you can't go home again. She locates Alex easily, can't help but smile at his rope tie, his patterned blazer with shoulder pads and the tapered sleeves pushed halfway up his arms. His boyish, unmeasured smile. He had been cute once, before she knew him. Such a perfect candidate, on paper. Jewish, a dentist, well traveled, well read. The kind of assumed confidence that comes from having screwed one's way unthinkingly straight through adolescence. She'd loved these things about him.

"You in one of these?"

The Cool Kid, next to her, reeks of CK One. She smells it at the same instant he speaks; springy and slimy, eau de teenage boy. It's the first question she's been asked about herself in a very long time.

"No," she tells him, smiling. "You?"

"Nah," he says. "Couple more years. If my mom makes me."

"I'm Dorit's aunt," Erin says.

"I'm Zac," says the kid. He stands there. She puts out her hand to shake, and he grabs it, hard. Someone has told him about the importance of a firm handshake.

"You a friend of Dorit's?" No, Erin, you moron, he's a party crasher.

"Sort of. Everyone has to invite everyone in the class. They made a rule."

"Did you already have yours?"

"Yup," he says. "In March."

"Get anything good?"

"Like four thousand bucks."

"*Jesus,*" she says.

"Yup."

"Wow. Times have changed." She loves that she just said this. Fucking loves.

"I guess."

After the service there are cookies and plastic shot glasses full of thick, sweet wine, and a photo op with the mottled silver kiddush cup Alex's grandfather had carted (barefoot, six thousand miles uphill both ways in the dead of winter) from Russia. Gertie has bonded with a small red-haired boy in shorts and suspenders, and they occupy themselves on the Henry and Rosalyn Biener Jungle Gym under the watchful eyes of Dorit's friends.

"*Mwah!*" Dana says loudly in the receiving line, pressing

her cheek to Erin's. "How nice to see you, hon." It's the "hon" that plucks on the electric harp of Erin's nerves.

"*Good* to see you," Nadiv says, clasping her hand in both of his. "*Great* to see you. *Good* to see you." He claps Alex on the back with a hairy paw and Alex reciprocates, a violent, manly hug in which only upper limbs touch. Never the torso. G-d forbid the torso. Or the hips, Lord Almighty.

"You were late," Dana says playfully to Alex, looking over his shoulder at the crowd still to be received.

Dorit leans over. "Yeah, Uncle Al—you guys showed up like halfway to the end, I saw you!"

"Gertie had an issue," Erin chimes in, to the interest of no one.

"I know," Alex says. "I know. I'm so sorry, Reetie. But we were just in time for your speech! You did such a great job. All that stuff about Abraham treating those strangers as well as he would treat God himself? Good stuff!" He insinuates himself into the receiving line and slings an arm around her. Dorit looks like she's about to have an aneurysm, resting her pink-pillboxed head against Alex's chest. Erin wanders away, stands off by herself. An ugly finger painting by little Dorit had adorned Alex's bachelor-pad fridge when he and Erin first met; she remembers thinking it was "adorable" and "a good sign" that he was so beloved an uncle. He'd tell Erin elaborate stories about his time with his niece—"And so I told her that God made rainbows but he also made bunnies who had to stop living sometimes, which seemed to really sink in, you know, because I want her to understand that life and death are two sides of the same coin, really, and I think she got it"—designed to showcase his highly developed, compassionate Way With Kids. Among Erin's coterie of husband-hunting girlfriends, this was a badge that ranked only slightly below Medical Degree or Paid Mortgage.

"Mommy! *Mom-meeee!* Mom! Me!" Gertie is atop the slide, a giant, flapping her arms gleefully like wings, her hands limp at the wrists. "Mommy!" You are my mother, she is saying. You! Are! My! Mother!, like an accusation. "Mommy!" People turn, grinning, to look at her, then at Erin. It's embarrassing, really. An unspeakably intimate, filthy relationship for all to see and think they understand. Erin wants to squirrel Gertie away, tuck her back into the womb where she'd again be a secret, aging in reverse peacefully right out of existence.

"What a *shtarker*," Nadiv booms with a wink. Erin takes this the wrong way, an implication that Gertie'll be a big fat dyke, someone Nadiv himself wouldn't want to fuck, wouldn't want as his trophy wife, a woman who won't engender the empowering sexual desperation necessary for the purchase of a house with an eight-tone doorbell. Which is simultaneously a compliment and, Erin thinks, given the world we live in, not.

"She's a terrible mother," Alex said in therapy the week before (or was it the week before that?), itemizing Erin's swearing, a stony if efficient response to a door-slammed finger, her (failed!) attempts to initiate sex while Gertie whimpered over the babycom.

Don't talk about me in the third person, she wanted to say. "My mother recently died," Erin had explained.

"That's not a Get Out of Jail Free card," Alex erupted. "She thinks that's a Get Out of Jail Free card! Her mother's been dying for *years!*" The therapist—her name is, no joke, Goodkiss—had had no clue what to say. She's a bad therapist, truly, but they've been seeing her for more than a year; the thought of starting over with someone new is exhausting and point-less. Which, actually, sums up pretty neatly Erin's reasons for having gotten married in the first place. Goodkiss just nodded, nodded, looked back and forth at them, nodded some more.

And Erin probably is a terrible mother. This is not to say that she doesn't love Gertie; that's hardwired—can't help lov-ing the little munchkin. But there is the feeling, the guilty, shameful, secret feeling, that she's stuck with her, that she would give her back in a heartbeat if she could, or at least leave her permanently in the care of someone else; someone competent and capable and trustworthy. Lately Erin is seized almost daily with the urge to live out of a van. In Texas, or Nashville, New Mexico; somewhere earthy and warm, some-where unexpected. She wants to become a massage therapist, live in a converted barn, become a vegetarian, try sleeping with women, learn the acoustic guitar, and start a band called Sarah Laughs or Everything But the Torah.

One of Dorit's contemporaries bounds up. "Omigod," she says. "Your little girl is *so* cute!" She's lanky and pretty and wearing too much lip liner.

"I know," says a second, an ill-fitting push-up bra cutting her breast buds diagonally in half. "What a cutie!" Newly pubescent girls always do this: one-up their not-so-distant playing of house by fetishizing real live small children.

"What's her name?" The first.

"Gertie."

"I love little kids with old-lady names! *Hi,* cutie!" she calls at the bottom of the slide, holding out her arms to Gertie, who eyes her suspiciously, chubby hands holding the railing tight.

The rabbi, holding a plastic cup of sweet wine and about five cookies stacked in his palm, comes over smiling. "Very cute little girl."

"Thanks," Erin says.

"How old?" He swallows a cookie practically whole.

"Sixteen months. Eighteen months. Sorry."

He chortles (indeed, with another whole cookie in his mouth; chortles). "Easy to lose track, huh?" Over in the receiving line Dana is *Mwah, mwah, mwah*-ing away, Dorit repeating "Thank you! Thank you! Thank you!", Nadiv lapsing into fast, loud Hebrew chatter with his relatives.

"Yeah," Erin replies, meaning it. She leans in. "I'm—was wondering," she says, impossibly meek and not wanting anyone to overhear. "Can you tell me what the Torah portion for the beginning of February would be? Or some portions from around then?"

"Oh," the rabbi says, third cookie inserted whole into the hole. "Well." This sounds like *Wow*, because of the cookie. She's holding her breath, she realizes, and slowly exhales, small increments of air, one at a time. "The Hebrew calendar doesn't work that way, you know; it doesn't correspond with the English calendar that way."

"Shit," she says, letting all the remaining air escape at once.

The rabbi laughs, jolly bastard. "What exactly do you want to know? I mean, what do you need to know?" He shoves another cookie into his face.

She looks over his shoulder, past his ear, which is sprouting little black hairs all along its rim. Alex is swinging Gertie in circles now, by her ankles, showing off for the girls. She'll puke, Erin thinks, or at the very least get all riled up and be impossible to put down for her nap. So be it, though: She will not play bad cop here, not in front of the rabbi and Dana and the Cool Kids, not on your life. Is this what makes her a bad mother? The willingness to let her munchkin throw up so she can win a probably half-invented power struggle with her fucking prick of a husband? Well, this is what happened when things deteriorated thusly. This would be the least of Gertie's suffering the consequences of Erin's idiotic choices. The rabbi is giving her that nice-rabbi look, that patient, rotund, hirsute learned-guy look.

"I guess it was like nineteen eighty-four . . . ," she trails off. Gertie is laughing hysterically, the kind of laughter that will, in about fifteen seconds, turn to sobs.

"Nineteen eighty-four?"

"My bat mitzvah," she tells him. And then—it feels kind of good to lay this down for him—"I forgot my *parsha*. I don't know what my *parsha* was."

"Ah," he says, fifth and final cookie disappearing into the hole. Is there a trace of disapproval there? There might be. There *should* be, she feels. But the rabbi just munches on his cookie, sanguine, nods.

"And," she adds, inexplicably, "my mother died last year."

Sure enough there comes at that moment an earth-shattering wail from Gertie. Erin, exhilarated, darts over and snatches her up, away from Alex, cradling her, whispering, "Shhhh" and "S'okay, little munchkin," smiling beatifically at concerned onlookers.

*   *   *

On the way home Gertie snores softly in the back, green dress rumpled, face covered with crumbs and chocolate from the remnants of a cookie she's still holding. The car has gotten extremely hot in the parking-lot sun, and Erin enjoys watching Alex sweat, enjoys watching him desperately futz with the AC.

"The rabbi said that there's tons of info about *parshas* on the Web," Erin says. "I gotta go online and figure out what mine was."

"Mmmm," Alex says after a second.

"It's just so weird that that memory's just gone, you know? Where did it go, you know?" She hates reaching out to him like this, but he's who's here.

"Mine was *Toldot*."

There is no getting around, at moments like this, the enormity of the deadness between them.

"I know." She looks out the window, watches as they pass a restaurant they'd eaten at once a few years ago and then never again. "What was *Toldot* about, anyway?"

Alex has both hands on the wheel, at ten o'clock and two o'clock, like they teach in drivers' ed. "Jacob and Esau," he says. His ever-expanding forehead is beaded grotesquely with sweat.

"No, I know," Erin says, attempting a playful slap on his arm. It's less playful than she intends. "But, really, I mean. What's it *about*? Do you remember?"

"Of course I remember."

"So?"

"Jacob and Esau!"

"But what *about* Jacob and Esau?" she asks. He puts his

hand over the vent, tries to turn to the AC knob higher than high. She starts to laugh. "You have no idea, do you? You dick." She should refrain from name-calling; it'll only get stockpiled in Alex's arsenal of therapy ammunition, only get hauled out for Goodkiss on Wednesday, but it's utterly worth it to her right now. The word, filling her mouth like a blunt object: *dick*. She laughs hard, from the gut. Wonderful, extended laughter.

"Leave me alone, Erin."

After careful deliberation Erin chooses a black jersey wraparound dress with three-quarter sleeves for the party. She'd worn it last to Sheila's funeral, and it still had, if she looked closely, pinholes from the small swatch of torn fabric they'd safety-pinned on to distinguish her as a mourner. She wishes she still had that ripped fabric, she wishes she could keep it pinned on, pass it off as nouveau fashion.

The dress deliberation is mostly an invented exercise; she has no other remotely appropriate party clothes that fit. Once upon a time she'd been a size eight; now, on the best of days, she's a twelve. She runs her hands over other dresses, old dresses, dresses she had worked once upon a time, but *Jesus,* what a baby did to the body! It was undoable. You had to be lithe and taut to live with another chick in a converted barn, waitressing between band practices, didn't you? You had to look cool not wearing a bra and not caring that you so happened to look hot. She is ineligible, now, she knows, for all of it. No matter, though; she'll wear her push-up bra and look somewhat okay at least from the waist up. The waist down is another matter entirely, and one she can do nothing about. The light would be soft and there'd be no Gertie and maybe she'd have a drink or two, maybe she'd dance.

Both Alex and Gertie are fast asleep, she in her crib and he on the couch in front of the TV, both drooling. Erin goes online, searches for "Torah Portion," and gets dozens upon dozens of sites. She starts with Chabad.org. This week's portion, it says, is *Vayeira*. She scrolls through an alphabetized list of every portion in the Torah, scanning them indiscriminately. They look a little familiar, all of them. From her own year of bar/bat mitzvahs all those years ago? From the well of some sort of collective unconscious? *Parsha in a Nutshell* is offered, then *Parsha in Depth. Commentary.* Last week was *Lech Lecha.* Next week it's *Chayei Sarah,* and then, what do you know?, *Toldot.* She clicks on *Parsha in a Nutshell.* Jacob and Esau, indeed. Fighting in Rebecca's womb for dominance, born into the world at odds. That striking image of wee Jacob gripping Esau's heel as he follows his brother out of the womb. Bookish Jacob's deception of old, blind Isaac while his strapping brother, Esau, is out hunting; two nations at odds evermore. It was true about the way people got set in their resentment and fury. Those things never go away, do they? They should make a movie out of this, Erin thinks; narratively it sure don't get much better.

She looks at a couple more (*Vayikra, Bamidbar, Shoftim*— why do they all sound somewhat familiar?) but gets restless pretty quickly. So after furtively getting up and shutting the door against her dozing family, she goes directly to teamgangbang.com, her porno site of choice. A relief to escape from the long list of familiar/foreign Torah portions. Alex's interest in sex had waned for a long time before dropping off completely to coincide with Gertie's arrival, and looking back, Erin can see that, of course, the teamgangbang.com began in direct response to the waning. Strange, she thinks, how long it can take for these things, these facts about one's own life, to take shape and assume a sensible form, incontrivable fact. For a good while, teamgangbang seemed an innocent enough (well, not in and of itself, obviously) substitute. It's all clear only from this vantage point: her willful blindness in marrying Alex, in settling for someone who doesn't love her, whom she doesn't love, her pigheadedness in proceeding, then, to get pregnant, to have the baby. To have the baby before her mother bit it, to have the baby so she wouldn't be so completely alone in the world. What vacuums these things were designed to fill. And how clear it all is to her now, *only now,* that they, the things, haven't succeeded whatsoever in doing so. On the computer screen, with the sound turned off, three gigantic black men pummel away at a bleached blond with two oversized nipple rings and five o'clock shadow pubic hair.

Erin thinks about cute Zac, the boy who'd top her "to do" list were she to be magically transported backward, back into herself as a young bat mitzvah debutante. She crosses her legs, rotates hips in desk chair, wonders if Dorit's friends are having sex yet. Erin certainly hadn't been—the dictum over the majority of her pubescence had been "everything but." Nothing else, nothing "but," was supposed to have counted.

*   *   *

77

Sarah arrives promptly at 6:45. Comes into the bathroom where Erin is almost finished applying makeup, perches on the counter. It's amazing, Erin thinks to herself, blowing on the blush brush, that she remembers how to do this.

Sarah grins. "What up, Erin?"

"Call me Mrs. Abrahms," Erin scowls, playing.

"Can I call you *Ms.* Abrahms?"

"Certainly *not*."

"Harrumph," says Sarah, inspecting an eye shadow as old as she is.

"Hey, Sarah, do you by any chance remember what your Torah portion was?" Erin flips her head over, gives her hair a few sprays, flips back up, looks like a disco queen. She hasn't gotten done up in forever, and the feeling is pretty nice. She once took this feeling for granted. Unbelievable.

"What, like, at my bat mitzvah?" Sarah is trying to dread her hair, which is blond and curly, but not quite kinky enough, so that a few months into the process it's still just a huge, smelly knot. Erin could not love her more.

"Yes, like at your bat mitzvah."

"Um," she says, following Erin into the living room. "The theme was 'Places I've Been'—which was like, Hawaii and Paris and the Grand Canyon on family vacations and Philadelphia to visit my grandparents and whatever. It was so fucking queer." She clamps her hand over her mouth, shakes her head, and looks over at Gertie, who's sitting in her bean-bag chair a foot from the TV, enthralled by the Teletubbies. *"Baaaaaaaaaa!"* says Tinky-Winky.

"But what was your Torah portion? What was your speech about?"

"Um . . . the Bible? I don't know."

Alex is jangling his keys by the front door. "Can we please not be late?"

Disregard for the time of others was yet another therapy topic. Erin can practically see the complaint taking shape, being given its very own brand-new file in Alex's deliberate little brain. *She's always late; she doesn't even try to make an effort. It was my niece's bat mitzvah, and she couldn't get it together to be on time.*

Go fuck yourself, Erin will say, or: *My mother just died.* Dr. Goodkiss will nod.

Erin kisses an oblivious Gertie, faces the mirror in the entry hall. Beige lip gloss, push-up bra, funeral dress all jazzy. Alex looks at her, says nothing. She waited months to broach the sexlessness with Goodkiss. She finds it deeply, deeply mortifying, has not told even her closest friends. She gazes longingly at Sarah, who's lying next to Gertie on the floor, doing her best Teletubbies impression for a *heh-heh-hehehe-heheh-*ing Gertie. Sarah would understand. Erin wants nothing (not even three enormous black dudes at once) so much as she wants to bow out of the bat mitzvah party and order in pizza with Sarah.

But, instead, since they're magically on time, since she's wearing a push-up bra, because today's combination of team-gangbang and parsha.com has filled her with all sorts of strange and familiar wanting, because in her better moments she believes wholeheartedly in the discipline of *Fake it 'till you make it,* and despite the presence of the empty, terrible car seat, Erin undoes her seat belt and leans over the parking break as Alex turns onto Wilshire.

"Hey," she whispers in his ear. He flinches as though a fly had grazed him, or a bee with a stinger. He keeps his eyes on the road. He's a good driver. Tense but pretty good: exactly what he's like as a lover. Erin kisses his neck. He likes this unequivocally, has always liked this. "Hey," she whispers again, feeling the jersey dress brush against her exfoliated knees, catching sight as she leans further down of her own shimmering, pushed-up cleavage. She slides a hand up his thigh.

"Erin," he says. "What are you doing?"

She continues the hand up his thigh, does a lap around his balls. For the life of her, she can't figure out the sexlessness. She's tried asking him. Is he cheating on her? Does he masturbate a lot, like she does? Did he just get old and stop caring? Was there a physical *problem*? She just wanted to know, she assured him. Whatever it was, it would be okay; she just wanted to *know*. He'd tried to get Goodkiss to back up the excuse that it was his Prozac, but she'd spoken, for once, these words from on high:

"Antidepressants can make it difficult to reach orgasm, but generally they help with the libido, they don't hinder it."

"She's only an LCSW," Alex had muttered on the way home from that appointment.

So recently Erin has tried to simply bypass Alex's brain. She'd wake up before him and put him in her mouth, just like all the women's magazines instructed. He'd jolt awake—*Goddammit, Erin, get off me!*—jump up and out of bed and into the bathroom. If she could just get him hard, she thinks, he'll remember what sex is like, how good it can be, how connective and fun. And he'll snap out of it, grab her, hold her tight, whisper dirty nothings in her ear. Until this occurs, Erin knows—*unless* it occurs—there is no hope for them. Because something was inexorably altered, something was lost forever, some capacity for friendship and parity between two people, when one had been known, with breathy, earnest seriousness at the height of passion, to beg the other to "shoot [his] cum inside [her]," and the other wouldn't so much as make eye contact.

She manages to get his fly unzipped partway, but he's squirming away from her, trying to keep his foot on the gas as he wriggles to the far edge of the driver's seat.

"Stop," he whines. She manages to somehow undo his pants entirely, to twist her hand down past the elastic of his boxer briefs, but then she gets snarled in his copious pubic hair. "Ow!"

He pulls over and puts the car in park just as she's grabbed hold of his penis. His *cock,* she'd called it giddily back when they used to fuck. She holds on to it stubbornly, ridiculously, even as he's trying to pull away, twist his body out of her reach, which, needless to say, is awkward, given the seat belts, the running engine, her grip. Not to mention the empty, terrible car seat.

"What are you *doing*? Jesus!"

Erin strains against him, aware only of her heaving bosom in the push-up bra, her own sweet-smelling skin, the way it would feel to be wanted like teamgangbang would want her. Then she lets go.

"What is *wrong* with you?"

"Jesus, Erin." He tucks himself back into his pants, pulls serenely back onto the road, hands placed precisely on the wheel. "Don't yell." Blood courses through her temples, boom, boom, boom like the *slap, slap, slap*ping of a good fuck.

She tried to rape me, he'll tell Goodkiss.

They follow a thumping bass line toward the ballroom at the far end of the hotel lobby, and are greeted by a bored coterie of kids standing around the place-card table.

"Par-*tay*," Alex tells them festively. They drift off and away. The thumping bass arranges itself all at once as the B-52s. "Love sha-a-ack, that's where it's at! Love sha-a-ack, that's where it's at!"

Mr. and Mrs. Alex Abrahms, first even among the As, are sitting at Eleanor of Aquitaine. This is preferable to Hillary Clinton, certainly, but a marked step beneath either Golda Meir or Madonna, Erin feels. The 'Great Women in History' theme is compromised slightly by a big black-and-white, glittery foam-board approximation of a scene marker by the ballroom entrance. In the space marked "production" is "Dorit's BM!" In the space marked "scene": 13. And in the space for "take" is, of course, 18, for *chai,* the collective lucky number of the Jews. Other than that brief, unavoidable foray into Hollywood (with the unintentional scatological overtone), it's "Great Women" in full effect. There's Queen Esther, Eleanor Roosevelt, Princess Di, Marilyn Monroe (perched hugely in cardboard relief above her demarcated table, trying half-assedly to keep that billowing white dress down), Marie Curie, even little Anne Frank. Who, Erin reasons, had indeed experienced the onset of menses, and so did indeed count. Joan of Arc, though, Erin takes issue with. Ditto Scarlett

O'Hara, who's fricking fictional. Plus, Erin's last name is not *Abrahms,* goddammit. Dana willfully ignores this, as a rule.

The ballroom is decked out in hysterics of glittering stream-ers, confetti, pink and white balloons, and looming Great Women. Face to face with a berobed Katharine Hepburn from *The Lion in Winter,* Erin unofficially gives up on the recollection of her Torah portion, sinks into a chair, and starts picking at the jelly beans scattered atop the table.

Also at Eleanor of Aquitaine are four other couples: all cousins but for Libby Pressman, Dana's best friend (a single mother of one) and her date. "It took me almost three years to get rid of my baby weight," she says to Erin by way of greeting.

The DJ, a short middle-aged man wearing hamburger-size earphones, turns on a mike, pumps a fist in the air. "Who's ready to *get down?*" The crowd lets out shrieks and a chorus of *Yeah*s. Then the lights flash, and a few strobes rotate wildly to the opening bars of "Eye of the Tiger." "Folks, let's put our hands together for the woman of the hour, she read from the Torah today, she's officially taken on the commandments, she's our very own bat mitzvah wo-*man,* she's *Dorrrr-Eeet!*"

And out she comes, to a standing ovation, her face shel-lacked with foundation and blush, and, Erin could swear, shadowing down each side of her only-a-matter-of-time nose, grinning madly and waving like Miss America. "Eye of the Tiger" segues into a hora. Alex sprints out onto the now-crowded dance floor and joins three others, grabbing one leg of a chair to hoist Dorit up into the air, her head coming dan-gerously close to the *R* of the huge pink D-O-R-I-T suspended from the ceiling. Substantial diamond studs in her ears catch the light spastically with every upward thrust of the chair.

Erin heads directly to the bar and orders a Jack-and-Coke, a throwback, the first drink she'd ever had ordered for her, the first drink she'd ever tasted on its way back up.

"What up, Auntie Erin?" Zac, it occurs to her, despite the parallel colloquial, is too young even for Sarah.

"Hey! Here." She hands him her Jack-and-Coke and signals to the bartender for another. Zac's face lights up.

"Cool!"

"*L'chaim!*" she fairly shouts before taking a hearty swallow. Zac looks left and right. "Cheers," he says, leaning in. He knocks the whole thing back. "Thanks."

"Go dance!" Erin tells him.

He curls a lip. "Riiiight. Why aren't *you* dancing?"

She shrugs, smiles coyly, motions for him to finish what's left of her drink and orders them two more.

In the sparkling handicapped bathroom off the other end of the lobby they're joined by two girls just growing into their growth spurts. One is a Gertie-fetishizer from earlier. They're impossibly lovely and improbably unthreatened by the presence of Erin, a bona fide adult, no getting around it. The girls plop down on the floor, not a thought for their dresses. Erin perches on the toilet, giggles nervously. On one level she's thrilled to have been included in this gathering, that old feeling of having been tapped for the inner sanctum making her feel strong and superior. All the other people, the ones *out there,* are losers. And on another level, well, it's hard to ignore the grownup issue.

Zac rolls a joint, licking the paper expertly.

"Nice," Erin says like an idiot. He passes it to her. Age before beauty, she thinks, sucking on it as he holds up an orange lighter.

"Dorit's a total dog," one of the girls comments, holding in smoke.

"Nasty," the other agrees.

The first exhales. "This party's la-ame."

"Totally," Erin says. "Amen!" These are her people. She takes the joint from Zac again. These people get her.

"The theme is gay."

"Emily Meltzner did the same thing." The first girl squints as she blows out a long, graceful stream. They all watch it disappear.

"What was yours?" Erin asks her.

"Sugar and Spice and Everything Nice," she says, folding her hands in her lap and batting her eyelashes prettily.

"Ha," says Erin. "And yours?" she nods at the other girl.

"Gardening." She fairly lights up, recalling it. "It was so cool. Each table was a different herb or something, and everyone at the table got some seeds to plant. . . . It was actually really cool."

"It actually was," Zac says, holding smoke. He coughs it out, and they laugh and laugh. Everything slows down, unravels: calm, linear, cloudless.

"What about you?" Erin sighs, flushed from all the laughing. She nudges Zac flirtatiously with her foot, which she's slipped out of her terribly outmoded black mules. The girls both have on these adorable ballet flats; the first's are covered with glitter and the second's are metallic gold.

"Basketball."

They all mull this for a moment. Into the empty space creeps Erin's awareness that she's in her late thirties with a crappy marriage and small child and dead mother and van-ished central memory of having been these kids' age, and she gives it the finger, closes her eyes, opens them again.

"I can remember everything about mine except my *parsha*," Erin says softly. "I had a Soviet twin and everything." When no one responds—did they hear her?—she wonders whether she spoke out loud. "Cute shoes!" she tells the girls. "Where'd you get them?"

"Oh," girl one says, looking at her feet. "Thanks. Fred Segal." Erin can't afford Fred Segal, not by a long shot.

"I love Fred Segal. Maybe if my fucking husband opened his own practice, I'd be able to shop there." She shakes her head, giggles, makes eye contact with girl two. "He's a dumb-fuck." Erin thinks about this, giggles some more. "Our mar-riage is totally, like, over." No one says anything. "We haven't had sex in like a year." The girls look at the floor.

"That sucks," someone says.

"Yeah," Erin says. "Omigod, did you guys see Dana? Do you believe what a complete idiot that woman is?"

"Who's Dana?" Zac relights the dwindling joint, sucks on it hard, flicks the lighter a few times.

"We should get back," girl one says.

"No!" Erin pleads. "Let's stay in here!" These are her friends. She likes it in here with them, the shiny surfaces and cool tile and expensive scented candle smell mixed with sweet weed, this inner, ageless sanctum. But they're getting up, looking in the mirror. Girl two takes a lip gloss out of her bra and touches up.

"Nah, we should really go back," Zac says.

"Pussies!" Erin blurts. They look at each other nervously. When they open the door she can hear the beat of the Electric Slide. They're leaving her, the assholes. She watches them helplessly from her perch on the toilet. She thought they were her pals. She has nobody.

"See you in there?" Cute Zac lingers briefly.

"Yeah."

"'Kay. See ya!"

When the door slams shut behind them, she gets up and relocks herself in, locks the strains of the Electric Slide out. Then she sits down on the floor where girl one had been, hugs her knees into her chest, and then rolls onto her side and curls up fetal.

She tries not to go back to wanting to remember her Torah portion, but the wanting is just there, unbidden. What was it, goddammit? Which one? The harder she tries to remember the less she'll be open to remembering, so she tries to avoid the wanting. The wanting is the problem, has always been the problem, will always be the problem. This, if she were sober, might inspire her to take a new tack with Alex. But she isn't sober, so it doesn't occur to her that way, and won't: not ever. She stretches out on the floor, on her back now, legs splayed. She thinks about tearing Alex a new asshole re: *Toldot*. She thinks about telling him, on the way home, everything she learned on Chabad.org, about claiming it that way for herself, as her own. But even what she read today has slipped away: Jacob and Esau, a birthright, deception, fighting, whatever. She tries to ignore the music from the ballroom, tries to avoid imaginings of the DJ dancing lamely, the leis and Glow Sticks and confetti circus of it all, the girls with socks slipped on over their hosiery for dancing. *Thriller,* the *YMCA,* Dana protesting speciously as they lift her up overhead in a chair.

She reaches up her dress and into her underwear, searching for a fantasy, a hook, running through the roster of what she's known: her bat mitzvah–era crushes, her high school boyfriend, her college love, strings of meaningless hookups, Alex, the specter of teamgangbang vs. some unfortunate wench, cute Zac—waiting for the wanting to alight on something worthwhile, something concrete enough to comprise a fantasy, something identifiably hers. But almost immediately she can feel that it's futile, that she has no orgasm in her, nothing to provoke the basis for an orgasm, nothing to hold on to and celebrate in that way, no memory good enough to help her get there, nothing to reach back for that would even get her close.

Spooked

I am useful in situations like these. Someone has died, and we are all gathered here, flies on shit, eating and talking, mindful to keep our voices low and somber. My mother is standing by a tray of cold cuts, shaking her head, her face full of sadness. My mother is good at this. Later she will tell me: "Brenda is not dealing properly. She needs to face reality sooner or later. I'll bring over some soup next week." But right now my mother is shaking her head and speaking softly to Brenda, the widow, her closest friend and once-upon-a-time sorority sister. Brenda seems like she's wondering what's happened, looking around her living room at all these familiar faces, until it rushes back and hits her squarely in the chest, a heavy, sticky awareness that spreads like syrup: Her husband, Howard, is dead.

My mother sort of knows this drill, sort of knows about the dead weight in Brenda's chest, sort of knows about trays and trays of cold cuts and bagels and pastries, about disbelief. My father left us when I was six, before I could form a lasting impression of him. All I have are blurry images of his black wingtips coming home from work, the feeling of his facial stubble against my chubby cheeks when he kissed me, vestiges of his funky-rancid smell after a set of push-ups on their bedroom floor on Sundays. We are closed off, my mother and I, and we do not discuss my father, whose name was Neil. He didn't die, but he's still gone, and I like to pretend he is dead. It's a lot simpler that way.

I wonder what I would have been like at six, in a similar roomful of sad and sympathetic people. Inappropriate, I bet, talking and laughing loudly, disturbing the reverie of people missing Neil. A six-year-old is a six-year-old, death in the family or no. Now that I'm older, I wish that I could really experience the loss of Neil. This time he would really be dead, and I would really feel it.

My mother comes over to me, ever helpful, exactly who you'd want at your dead husband's *shiva,* to ask if I wouldn't mind taking Tulip for a walk. Tulip is lying in the corner of the room, and she lifts a bored eyebrow at the sound of her name, but makes no movement. I don't know what kind of dog she is, but she always seems depressed and a little bit sick, with crusty eye boogers and a kind of socky smell. "She hasn't been walked since it happened," my mother tells me. "Danny's too upset to have to think about this now. It would be such a help, Jilly, please?" Like I said: I am useful in situations like these. Appropriate, on call.

I like pretending that Tulip is my dog, that this is my house we are leaving to go on our walk, that it is Neil who died the day before yesterday, that it is my time to be sad about Neil. I would really like to be the kind of person who has a dog, who walks the dog, who wears these sleek black funeral clothes with such grace and ease on a sunny afternoon walk around the block, whose dad is actually dead and not just gone.

So I invent: My name is Juanita and I have eight brothers and sisters and a concave stomach and a boyfriend in the eleventh grade, in a band. And then I revise: It is *my* father who is dead today, and I have cried with restrained fury and sorrow all morning, I am exhausted with the effort it took to make it through, and now I am on a walk with my faithful only friend, Tulip.

It strikes me suddenly that I am walking the dead man's dog. How close I am to the dead man himself! My father was allergic to dogs, but what if we'd had one? Then there'd be something left, a direct link to Neil. Neil's best friend. The leash yanks Tulip slightly backward as I come to a near stop, making it seem as if she were flinching at something or some-one. A ghost, perhaps: Howard, dancing, twirling, floating up to some clear-arteried heaven.

This is a nice neighborhood. "Nouveau riche," my mother hissed at me as we drove through here earlier today. Our neighborhood is older, not as repetitive and planned as this one. "The landscaping says it all," she said, flat and harsh as the street itself. She said she couldn't understand why Brenda and Howard would choose to move here, to this provincial suburban nightmare of wide sidewalks and wider-open spaces above and around each pink pastry of a house. Good schools for Danny or no.

But everything seems even and right as I walk with Tulip. I imagine that Tulip and I are in a play. The scenery behind us, painted on a long sheet of butcher paper like the kind they used to cover the tables during art in kindergarten, is rolling by slowly while we move our legs in place. It is a stage trick, an illusion. It is better than reality.

Truthfully I half-expected Danny to fall into my arms this morning. I really wouldn't have minded if he'd buried his head in my breast and gotten snot on my dress in a fit of anguish. It stung, like a stubbed toe, when he looked past me, eyes focused on some distant, fascinating point, and only nodded slightly at my mother. I wished I didn't know him in his dark gray suit, so that I could look at him and not see him at nine, picking his nose. I wished I could take him out of context. The sight of him (serious as a heart attack, trying to keep his balance while sidestepping headstones) pinned me to myself, made me claustrophobic, closed up in a plain pine box for good. It's hard to take death seriously in the thick of it. Years of TV funerals take over and play themselves out: the downcast mouths, subdued gestures, understanding nods. I looked at the sky, I wondered if I still had any lipstick on, I pretended we were burying a time capsule.

My own father's departure was too long ago to be of any benefit to me now, and it wasn't even the right kind of departure. I get no sympathy when it matters; none of my high school teachers put their arms around me and tell me to finish my American History paper whenever I can, no rush. But I still want the clout I deserve. *My father's gone, too,* I fiercely and silently tell Danny. *Don't think you're the only one.* But he ignored me this morning, standing off by himself a bit, body language telling everyone to fuck off.

"Danny needs to learn that he does not have a monopoly on tragedy," said my mother on the way through the gates of the cemetery; the worst over, the Mexican men left to pile dirt onto the casket, each *thwack!* of earth on wood like a heartbeat in the sinuses when you have a headache.

Danny looked a lot like his dead father. I thought it might make sense for my mother to envy Brenda that, a dead ringer for her dead husband. Dead, dead, dead, dead, I have to keep reminding myself. I'm finding it necessary to rehash Howard in my head: a father, a husband, a wearer of arrow-collar polyester shirts, bemoaner of conservative politics. He grew his hair long in the back to reimburse his ego for the thinning on top. I remembered him commenting on my breasts a few times (*Filling out nicely, aren't we, Jill?*). Dead of a heart attack at fifty-something. Survived by a wife and a look-alike adolescent son and indifferent, confused dog wondering at abandonment and the smell of the hand that fed her.

My reverie ends abruptly when Tulip squats and begins to pee in some shrubbery. "Tulip," I say, "where are your manners?"

Then I am no longer Juanita, I am Jill. And I don't have any siblings, it's just me and my mother in our musty, formal dining room, eating dinner on weeknights in silence. And my father isn't dead, he's just gone. And this is a dead man's dog relieving herself in someone's ficus. All at once I am sweaty and my back hurts and I realize we have been gone a while. I feel illogically as if I will be in trouble.

A brief but spectacular wave of panic submerges me: *Where am I?* These houses all look the same and it's weirdly quiet. I turn in a slow circle, trying to orient myself by a lawn ornament, an unusually colored car, someone else in black, maybe carrying an aluminum-foiled casserole for the freezer of the dead man's family. But it is so quiet. I give Tulip's leash a yank and she reluctantly follows me. I am in a hurry now.

It is comical to be scurrying along calm suburban sidewalks like a city secretary in sneakers and stockings on her way to work, arms pumping. Tulip knows how comical it is, and she mocks me with her limp, bouncing tongue. But I am looking, looking, looking for something that will tell me how to get back to the dead man's house and the dead man's mourners. Perhaps I myself would not be missed, but Tulip is a faithful friend, and she is needed at that house, by those mourners.

I round corners with ridiculous intensity, like a medieval adventurer in a maze, making haphazard decisions that will lead me nowhere.

I end up on a fairly busy large street. There are three lanes in each direction on either side of a long, thin concrete island. The houses that stand defiantly facing this street look battered and brave, like people who refuse to take Prozac. The suburban dream of a few blocks past seems theoretical, phony, cowardly.

I am still confused and worried about finding my way back, imagining Danny looking for his dead father's dog and not finding her, but the *whoosh!* of passing cars lulls me into complacency, and I ease back into a stroll, thinking: Fuck Danny. I deserve a dog, too.

Tulip does not seem to like the cars and the noise and the haste of this street. She is a product of fraudulent tranquillity, and this is all too much, too fast. So she begins to run, faster than she would on a precoronary morning jog with Howard, the dead man. She runs faster now than she would on the familiar, suburban streets that really are just a few blocks away from this honking, this tailpipe stench, this foolish race toward the next red light. She runs faster than I can, although I try, sweaty and hopeless, the strap of her leash welting my right palm. She is spooked, and I allow myself to hope for a split second that sandpaper-faced, sweetly stinking Neil will show up in a white robe or something, and shoot her.

I can't keep up. My chest feels tight and too small, like Brenda's today, like my mother's might have, way back when, if only Neil had died. I let go of the leash and feel free, weightless, as if I've stepped onto a moving sidewalk. Tulip runs on, looking beautiful and completely out of place, her golden ears and leash flapping behind her as she gallops down the street, until I can no longer see her. And then I feel catheterized and clean. There is a blossoming somewhere near my heart full of relief and pain, eclipsing worry. Tulip is gone, and I am left with this weightlessness, the passing cars like the sound of an intense wind. My mother's voice is as clear as water: *She could get hit by a car. What if she can't find her way home? For God's sake, Jill, why can't you do anything right? Howard had that dog for years.* And then she is quieted by a huge passing truck and a trail of brown exhaust, which also disappears.

I walk on and imagine Danny looking for Tulip, wanting some silent, supportive canine company, Danny finding Tulip gone, Danny freaking out, throwing platters of cookies at startled guests, Danny losing father and dog all at once, death upon death, like a mathematical problem: loss squared. My mother will wonder why she didn't just leave me by the coffeepot and butter cookies, why she insisted on making me useful. Brenda will stand by the window with a nervous-oblivious smile on her face and her eyes immutable and think: It's such a nice day outside, somebody ought to take Tulip for a walk.

How This Night Is Different

After halfheartedly helping her mother clean, sweep, launder, and dust ritually with a feather and a candle borrowed from the emergency earthquake kit, Joanna congregated with her parents on the patio. They stood around a mop bucket and beamed at her.

"Jo-Jo," her father said, the same way he'd said it when she was eight. "Show us what you found."

Joanna held up the *hametz*: a quartered piece of white bread Ron had "hidden" for her to "find" (smack in the middle of the dining room table, on top of the microwave, on top of the washing machine, and by the kitchen sink, respectively). He nodded approvingly and flipped through the Haggadah for the appropriate blessing. He read it first in Hebrew and then in English.

"Any leaven in my possession, which I have not seen or removed, shall be as if it does not exist, and as the *dust* of *earth*." To this last part, "the *dust* of *earth*," Ron added a sinister and dramatic flourish, so it sounded almost as if he was promising, when he found you, to *suck* your *blood*.

The quartered bread sat soggy and rejected in Joanna's sweaty open palm. On the inside of her left forearm the tattooed words "why" and "not" unfolded in small blue-black Times New Roman italics, followed by an outsize question mark. The words had been meaningful to her when she'd gotten them at twenty-three but had long since ceased to mean whatever they had meant, and had had no choice, then, but to assume new meanings as she grew ever older looking at them every day. She saw her mother try not to stare. Usually Joanna made a point of long sleeves in the presence of the 'rents, to spare them all the torment.

"An Orthodox guy in Pico-Robertson accidentally set himself on fire doing this last year," Joanna informed them. Then she dropped the bread into the bucket and Marilyn lit a match. For a little while they watched the flame do its worst, until the stench of burned toast forced them back inside. The bucket remained out on the patio all day, blackened quarters disintegrated at the bottom.

Joanna was home for the *sedarim* so, of course, the task of setting the table fell to her. Wasn't it a given for adult children to fall immediately back into their preordained roles within the family upon returning home? And look at that: "home"! Still, forever, she found herself referring to her parents' house—a place she'd left decisively at seventeen—as *home*.

Once upon a time there had been no greater pleasure than in her imagined grownup responsibility of making the table "look pretty," but she was a ripe thirty-one now, a ways away from eleven. And as she unpacked her grandma Bess's ancient, precious Passover china from its musty foam crate, she smiled at the memory of her mother's sly manipulation: *It's your job to make the table look pretty, Jo-Jo!* Once upon a time she had relished the assignment. She would fuss about the precise angle and distance of the wine glass from plate and knife, feel betrayed when guests actually sat down to eat, messed up her perfect settings, ringed the crystal with lipstick.

After a couple of rocky periods in her twenties (a few particularly bad breakups, a pinch of credit card debt, unceremonious abandonment of a master's in painting, enforced leaving—okay, so she was fucking her boss—of a plum graphic design job, bridges thoroughly charred), Joanna seemed now to have her "shit" more or less "together," as they say, and her proficiency in making the table *look pretty* seemed proof enough. She set each plate so that the stem of its centered red poppy extended downward. This, she recalled from Marilyn's formative instruction, was an important detail: gravity applied in the aesthetic of fine china. She cared considerably less these days about place-setting precision, but she would not betray the girl she had been. Evenly spaced flatware was the other crucial thing.

When the foam china crate was empty, though, and there were only *eleven* delicate red poppies flowering within thick navy blue borders ringed with gold leaf evenly spaced around the table, Joanna felt defeated. The twelfth plate, she fully recalled, had been broken during a raucous party she had hosted in eleventh grade. Josh Weinstein, her first love, had raided the pantry looking for snacks. Joanna had been completely, blessedly stoned, and, needless to say, pretty hungry herself, so she'd just let out a spacey giggle when Josh emerged onto the patio with a Grandma Bess Passover plate instead, palming the red poppy like an affected French waiter.

"Zees ees niiiice," he'd said, making ridiculous faces at Joanna. (They'd dated all through high school and into college, but he'd ended up being a total fucker; cheated on her for months, left her at the end of freshman year with a parting gift of genital warts.)

Jay Taubman, from a couple dozen feet away, had clapped his gigantic pubescent paws and held them out—"Dude! Right here!"—and Josh had tossed the blue-rimmed artifact as if it were a Frisbee. It had sailed for what seemed like hours, spinning gracefully through the air toward Jay.

"Wait," Joanna had said weakly. "Don't." But then there had been a shatter, the onomatopoeic pleasure of which reverberated sharply in the ganja-tinged pit of her stomach. She remembered having giggled in spite of herself. *Crash!* Tee-hee.

"Mom," she said, slouching into the kitchen, "Grandma Bess's Passover china only has eleven plates."

"Where's the twelfth?" Marilyn, wrist deep in a bowl of nuts and cinnamon and finely chopped apples for *charoset*, raised an eyebrow.

Joanna shrugged, looked at the floor. "I have no idea." Usually they went to Aunt Barbi and Uncle Larry's for Passover.

"So just use a plate from another set," Marilyn said, furiously mixing. "The pink flowers one. Honestly, Joanna. Things break. It's not the end of the world."

"Who said anything about it breaking?" Joanna's voice veered dangerously into the realm of shrill. She had expected her mother to be more upset. Grandma Bess had died before Joanna's birth—had not lived to see her first grandchild—and Joanna always felt it was a huge deal when things broke. The end of the world, even. Marilyn kept on mixing. "Why would

I have any idea what happened to the freaking plate?" Marilyn said nothing. "What the *hell?* I don't even *live* here. Jesus."

Joanna's emotional susceptibility was aggravated by the raw, itchy, extraordinarily uncomfortable state of her genitalia: a yeast infection, for sure, noticed the day before in its earliest stages and blossomed to full, awful effect today. It was driving her insane; she wanted to rip into her vagina with an ax, to tear it apart and revel in the ecstasy of the itch relieved. She had a Problem in her Pants, as the girls in her co-op in college used to say. There were proliferate Problems in their Pants back in the day: UTIs, various and sundry STDs, yeast. "Curse the motherfucking Pill," her friend Claire would moan, knocking back shots of not-from-concentrate cranberry juice at the kitchen table. "Sexual liberation comes with a hefty price tag indeed, ladies."

"That china was Grandma's dowry when she married your grandpa Jack," Marilyn said after a moment, like amusing, disconnected trivia. Grandpa Jack was, naturally, even longer gone than his blushing bride. There was a picture of them, fingers intertwined, sepia cheeks pressed delightedly together, dressed to the nines, about to leave on their honeymoon, front and center on top of the baby grand in the living room. It was as disquieting an image as any flayed and emaciated Catholic Jesus-on-the-cross: They had died for Joanna's sins.

Marilyn briefly consulted her recipe, pulled nutmeg off the spice rack, and added two decisive shakes to the bowl. *Charoset* was Joanna's favorite part of Passover by far. More even than the little individual dipping bowls of saltwater meant to approximate tears.

"I'm sorry, Mom!" she said suddenly, attempting, in an off-center hug, to bury her face in Marilyn's shoulder. "I'm so sorry!" It seemed to Joanna that the missing twelfth plate should somehow exacerbate her mother's old mother-loss wound, twist and wring her psyche, and dredge up all the pain of losing one's mother—being, in fact, an orphan—might entail. Joanna couldn't imagine it: God dead. Marilyn gave her a friendly little shove.

"Would you please spare us the drama and finish setting the table? Fifty people are going to be here in a half hour and You. Are. Not. Helping. Me." This was punctuated by the shaking of her hands over the mixing bowl, as though the bits of spiced apples and nuts sticking to her fingers were them-selves being selfish. When she was expecting company, Mar-ilyn tended toward hyperbole and (dare we?) hysteria. The Renaissance painters had missed a sprawling goldmine when they'd neglected to portray the Martyrdom of the Put-Upon Passover Seder Hostess. There were exactly twelve people coming: Aunt Barbi and the axis of asshole (Uncle Larry and cousins Kevin and Jason), sad-sack still-single Uncle Steve, Aunt Jackie and her silent, obese boyfriend Bob, studying-for-about-six-years-now-to-become-a-beautician cousin Stacey, Joanna, Marilyn, and Ron. And Harris. Joanna's boyfriend of almost a year. A non-Jew. ("I don't like to be defined by what I'm not," he would mock bristle at that. "I'm also a nonmidget. A non-Hispanic. A nonfemale." "And a nonnonagenarian," Joanna would point out, because, like her, Harris had a dumb sense of humor. "Ha," he'd respond. "You said 'nonnonagenar-ian.'" Then they would talk about other things.)

So Joanna reluctantly got out a plate from the grotesque second-tier Passover set—ceramic yellow with pretty pink daisies. It looked obscene, a monstrosity among all of Grandma Bess's serene, expensive red poppies. Like a hooker at high tea. She set it at her own place, disgusted by the awful aesthetic of it, then allowed herself a quick, feral itching interlude, hand down the waist of her jeans, facing the corner of the dining room, hunched over like a pervert jerking off in public. The reprieve was borderline orgasmic—she saw rainbows, she saw stars—with a nice little thread of pain sliced through like gold leaf. She let out a small involuntary sigh and examined her fingers: white, pasty, not altogether too heinous smelling, considering.

In the kitchen Marilyn was racing around like Julia Child on crack.

"All right," Joanna told her. "The table is set. Can I be excused?" Instantly she regretted the sarcasm in her voice. Marilyn made a big show of rinsing her hands off and drying them on a dishtowel, which she then folded decisively in quarters and set down next to the sink. Joanna leaned against the counter, arms crossed, directly in her mother's path. "I really hope you're not expecting me to say the Four Questions, because I'm fucking thirty-one years old and it's not happening."

"I know how old you are." This with a defeated tone, in which Joanna could hear each and every one of her mother's many harbored disappointments: an only child, unmarried, dating a goy, spectacularly unaccomplished in her chosen craft, living far away, tattooed, still accepting the occasional bailout check from Daddy. The list went on. Breaker of plates, eschewer of intergenerational cultural responsibility, what else?

"Good," Joanna replied, like a nine-year-old. She had expected more of a fight, and didn't know what to do with her reserve of belligerence. Her crotch burned.

"Maybe your friend Harris can do it," said Marilyn. "That would be appropriate, don't you think?" At which the doorbell rang.

"Elijah!" Ron yelled from the den, where he was doing roughly ten times the necessary Seder prep: cutting and pasting readings from eight different *Haggadot,* making place cards (which he would any minute ask Joanna to illustrate "because you're the talented artist, Jo-Jo"), assigning roles in the skit wherein Moses asks pharaoh to pretty please Let [His] People Go. Sweet Ron got such immense pleasure from the claim that anyone at the door on Passover was, in fact, Elijah. It never got old. For the rest of the evening, whenever the doorbell rang, he would invariably pause, straight faced, dopey, joyful, before making the joke anew.

"I expect you to wear long sleeves to the table, Joanna," Marilyn said, her parting shot. "Please don't make everyone uncomfortable."

"Yeah, sure, why not?"

Joanna opened the front door, and Harris—*Oh, Harris!*—held out the urgently requested box of Monistat 7 and a pretty bunch of yellow tulips. "Hell-o," he said too brightly, doing a little bow as if they were meeting for the first time. Behind him the afternoon was ending, and the light was prismatic and warm, like in a well-taken photograph on specifically appropriate film. Joanna felt a little joy hiccup bubble up her center. Her very own bass-and-drums-playing borderline-hippie college football champion. The Gentle Giant, Joanna's friends called him. He had gifted her with a painstakingly compiled homemade CD mix on their second date, full of all sorts of hidden, funny references to things they had talked about on their first, some of which she was still decoding. He was perfect in bed: ravenous, unshockable, but not the slightest bit sleazy. Did such men really exist?

"Why, thank you," she said, taking the tulips and the Monistat (which effected, downstairs, an anticipatory wave of relief) with a ladylike curtsy.

He raked a hand through his hair (sand colored, shaggy, lovely) and stepped over the threshold. "Do I look okay?" Brown Hush Puppies, khakis, an untucked periwinkle blue shirt unbuttoned to reveal the white T-shirt underneath. Joanna, at five ten, came up to his chest, which was, for a tall girl, a sexual intoxicant like no other. He could have worn Italian slides and Lycra, it didn't matter. She could not have been more attracted to him. It was like a sickness.

"Perfect," she told him. "Beautiful. Don't be nervous."

"Who's nervous?" He shrugged, pretended to look over his shoulder, wrapped his arms around her. When he kissed her she felt *that thing*—that thing she might have identified as love, as happiness, had she any concrete previous experience with either to which she could yoke it.

After Josh "the Warthog" Weinstein, there had been a whole string of schmucks, Nice Jewish Narcissists all. All these guys were the same: lionized beyond repair by doltish, worshipful mothers, interested ultimately in doltish, worshipful girlfriends-cum-wives. These boys invariably rejected the hell out of her (being, as she was, neither doltish nor particularly worshipful), and in return, she developed a steaming, pulsating, wholly unwieldy contempt for the summer-camp-

whoring lot of them. Joanna had shed actual tears in a therapist's office when she was twenty-eight, after yet another dis-
astrous go at homoethnic dating. "I'm an anti-Semite," she'd
sobbed in response to the standard "Why are you here?" "I
hate Jews." The therapist had recommended both *Women
Who Love Too Much* and *Portnoy's Complaint* and sent
Joanna on her way.

Harris had been a regular at the Near Miss, Joanna's coffee
shop in Berkeley. She worked afternoons to closing. He ran a
recording studio nearby, she found out later, and would stum-
ble in at noon, read the paper, go to work at two or three.

"Is he Jewish?" Naturally, Marilyn's first question.

"From one of the lost tribes, I think," Joanna had replied.
"Kind of like a Jew for Jesus, but minus the Jew part."

"Oh, Joanna." Marilyn cared obsessively about Jewish
boyfriends (and husbands and grandkiddies, natch); Joanna
cared about unbroken inherited china. Two sides of the same
coin, it did not escape Joanna's perception, but they stared at
each other in willful mutual incomprehension nonetheless.
"Bess is turning over in her grave." Grandma of the Shattered
Plate: patron Jew of guilt and shame.

"How can she dislike me when she doesn't even know
me?" Harris would ask, genuinely hurt and confused.

"Nobody dislikes you," Joanna would explain. "Jews are
just a little defensive about blood thinning. It's been a rough
couple of thousand years." His family treated Joanna with a
healthy mixture of skepticism (borne of an inkling that there
existed sentiment in Joanna's family that Harris was somehow not good enough for her) and welcoming openness, man-
ifested in their eagerness to add a red-papered box with her

name on it under their massive Christmas tree, their place-ment of a framed picture of her and Harris to their already overcrowded mantel.

"Your very first seder," Joanna told him upstairs in her childhood bedroom, trying on varieties of outfits that would not further harsh her crotch. The Monistat wasn't so very *stat,* after all—it would take at least a day until she'd feel any relief. She'd have to go commando, no question. Let it breathe. Marilyn used to say that, an admonishment never to wear underwear to bed. *Your vagina needs to breathe,* Joanna, covers pulled to her chin, could recall hearing in lieu of a bedtime story. A pretty disconcerting image for a little girl, needless to say—she had feared for years that she was smothering her vagina under clothes all day, that the beast of it (teeth and all) was gasping for air under her jeans. She'd taken fastidiously in high school to a pair of deliciously ratty, paint-splattered denim overalls, roomy in the crotch, which she still wore. Roomy in the crotch had come to be, in fact, a central tenet of Joanna's fashion sense.

"I've been to a seder before," Harris said, mock outraged, though no, of course he hadn't. He'd bought out their neigh-borhood bookstore of Harold Kushner, stopped mixing dairy and meat, started peppering his speech with Yiddishisms, ex-pressed huge retroactive gratitude for the perfunctory cir-cumcision performed on multitudes of male infants born in urban hospitals in the early seventies. "The retelling of our emancipation from slavery gets me all *farklempt* every time." He wiped away a *faux* tear. The absurdity of finding a philosemite here, in her life! She had suggested that they sim-ply skip Passover, stay in Berkeley, go out for Indian, what did she care? But *noooo,* Harris wanted to "experience" it, home-style.

"It's the longest, most boring holiday ever," she'd told him. "It's the worst. You get constipated, you get sick on bad wine, you talk biblical mythology until everyone nods off in their bone-dry matzo cake. I promise, it sucks!" He wouldn't hear any of it.

"I want to show you that I'm amenable to Judaism," he'd said.

"I believe that's the official motto of post–World War II Europe, honey," she'd retorted. And here they were.

"I'm not feeling so hot," she said, forgoing the notion of pants entirely. She stepped into a red silk skirt, then back out of it when she remembered she'd be wearing no underwear. Then back into it when she realized who gave a fuck. A cool breeze fanned the flame of her womanhood. She relished the air.

Harris opened his messenger bag, removed a bottle of Coke. "You look ravishing." He took a swig. "Not a winner," he sighed, glancing at the underside of the cap.

"Fuck, Harris, I don't think Coke is kosher for Passover." But neither was she at the moment, with yeast multiplying exponentially in her crotch, maybe enough by now to bake a loaf or two of forbidden bread. Though she was half afraid to explain this particular aspect of the ailment, unsure she wouldn't be sold out by gung-ho Harris and then hunted down with candle and feather by Marilyn, ejected immediately and unceremoniously from the house: revealed to be very, very unkosher for Passover.

He froze, mid sip, looked left and right. "Um. What do we do?"

"Just give it to me. Here." She screwed the top back on and then put the bottle in the cabinet below the sink in her bathroom, with crusted hair defrizz and twelve-year-old sunblock.

"I'm sorry! Should I, like, shower or something?" He seemed to really want to be part of this thing, this random set of rules with no connection to him whatsoever.

"I think you're okay, babe."

"Or brush my teeth?"

"Harris. No one has to know. It's fine. We'll just keep this between us."

"But I'll know."

She held her hand up in front of his face and waved it around a couple of times. "There, now I've absolved you. That's how it works. You're clean." She crossed herself, did some half-recalled sign language from when that deaf lady with the perm guest-starred on *Sesame Street,* and flipped him the bird.

"I love you," he said. They stretched out on her old trundle bed with white aluminum curlicue frame. He was huge, a bear. He enveloped her entirely, radiating warmth like clothes fresh from the dryer.

"Don't," she told him when he slid his hand from between her knees up under the skirt. "Problem in my pants."

"Ah, yes," he said. "I forgot. Sorry. Me too." He amiably directed her hand to his hard-on.

They lay there together, breathing slowly, listening to the doorbell ring and to Ron shouting "Elijah" and to Marilyn speciously chirping, "Hel-*lo!* Come in!" After a few minutes, Joanna untangled herself halfway to grab a felt-tip pen and illustrate Ron's place cards. When she was satisfied with her appropriation and representations of blood (Aunt Barbi), frogs (Stacey), vermin (Kevin), wild beasts (Uncle Larry), pestilence (Jason), boils (Aunt Jackie), hail (Bob), locusts (Uncle Steve), darkness (Ron), and slaying of the firstborn (Marilyn), she reconstituted herself into Harris's embrace and softly gnawed his thumb pad. There weren't enough plagues to go around, and since Harris was a newbie and she herself was currently afflicted with one even the fucking Egyptians had been spared, Joanna had just drawn little fat balloon hearts on Harris's place card and a little personified grinning sun on her own.

"Ready to face the enemy?"

He scowled. "My ancestors could've blood-libeled yours into oblivion."

"Let's go," she said, opening her bedroom door. "We're gonna get totally shit-faced on Manischewitz. It's, like, mandated."

Harris followed her down the stairs and into the living room.

"Here she is . . . ," boomed Ron, the opening of "Miss America."

And there *they* all were, sitting or leaning on the beige L-shaped sofa: the sum total of Joanna's familial relations. Marilyn was an only child, so that line dead-ended with Joanna. Ron's three siblings, Barbi, Steve, and Jackie, were, respectively: a type-A bitch on wheels, a sociopathic loner, and a chronically ill codependent. And the next generation? Kevin and Jason, MIT grads who always referred to Joanna's forte as "arts and crafts" and pretended to forget the name of the state school she'd attended; and Stacey, a developmentally disabled mama's girl, living at home, thrilled to death at thirty-five with the possibility of getting licensed to do nails. Ten pairs of eyes fixed on Harris.

"Hi," he said, like a champ, with a doleful wave it would be impossible not to love, Joanna thought.

"This is Harris," she said. Everyone nodded politely and took note of Harris, the goy. For shame. And Joanna an only child. And *Marilyn* an only child. The Jewish people would die out, and whose fault was it? She handed the place cards ("plague cards," he called them) off to Ron.

Harris didn't quite get that upon meeting Joanna's family he would indeed be defined solely by what he was not. He also didn't get what so depressed Joanna about this gathering, this particular grouping of people. "As if their meager numbers weren't sad enough . . . ," she'd explained. "It's terrible. They're all such losers, and there are so few *of* them."

"This is Joanna's friend, Harris," Marilyn said, redundant, and then the whole room finally jumped to life with *hello, how nice to finally, welcome, hey there.* Kevin and Jason, smirking, caught Joanna's eye from across the room and shook their heads unhurriedly, side to side, implied tongues clicking.

Joanna had to summon up every iota of social fear and control in her being to keep from reaching down the waist of her skirt and scratching, scratching, scratching some more. She plopped loudly and ungracefully down on the couch, hoping contact would alleviate some of the distress.

Dr. Brooks, her pediatrician, had once stuck a finger all the way up inside her during a routine checkup when she was, who knows, maybe nine.

"Don't ever let anyone do that to you," he'd said to her after a brief moment, making her look him in the eyes. "If anyone ever tries to do that to you, you don't let them. You tell a grownup. Understand?" He kept staring at her, insistent, until she nodded, finally, slowly, mortified. But, she thought later, in the car with Marilyn, confused and still—still!—absolutely mortified, his words ringing in her ears and the feeling of his huge cold finger lingering, *he* had done it to her. Did that count or didn't it?

She had sunk into the passenger seat next to her mother that day, blistering shame, positive that there was something different, something noticeable about her that would bring on castigation and exile. She was shocked (and lonely, oddly, a new feeling that threw a net over her and dragged her away from the girl she thought she was) when Marilyn had seemed not to notice a thing, and had only suggested blithely that they go get an ice cream cone.

Aunt Jackie came over and laid a loud smooch on Joanna's cheek.

"Hey, Aunt Jackie."

"He seems nice."

"He is."

An old painting of Joanna's hung above them, a Chagall rip-off from grad school.

"Still painting, sweetheart?"

"Not really. Sometimes."

"That's a shame. You were so talented."

"I'm still talented," Joanna said. "Just not actively."

"Candles!" Marilyn called. "Ladies." Joanna and Jackie joined Barbi and Stacey by the buffet and they lit the candles. Jackie sang the blessing in a high-pitched vibrato, doing her best Joni Mitchell on the transliteration Marilyn gave her.

At the table everyone found their place cards and stood behind their chairs awaiting instruction. Joanna's mismatched setting (so yellow, so overtaken by daisies a shade of pink last seen in the era of punk, so loud and unseemly) languished amid the stately, banded Grandma Bess's, set her incontrovertibly apart. The travesty of the broken plate and its larger implications of wholeness defiled within the twelve-set dreams of her late grandmother, was further implicated in the raw and extraordinarily uncomfortable state of her genitalia. The maternal line, the whole fertility arena, the way, when Joanna clamped her thighs together, desperate for some friction, everyone else's red poppies swam together like healthy Georgia O'Keeffe twats in miniature.

"Oh, is that cute," Aunt Barbi held up her plague card, squinting. "Joanna, this must be your handiwork." Joanna had, for Blood, done a little cartoon Lady Macbeth, furiously attacking her hand, "Out, damned spot," in a speech bubble.

Harris had been placed across from Joanna, and he smiled at her now over the perfectly laid table, just the two of them, apart and distant from this family. They would start their own. "So talented," he mouthed at her.

"Well," said Marilyn. "Welcome to our seder. We're so glad to have you all *here* this year." Barbi reined in a nasty tight-lipped smile.

"We're so glad to be here, Aunt Marilyn." Stacey was wearing a dress that made Joanna's plate cower in floral fever pitch, her nails done in a pattern to match.

"Sit, sit, everyone sit." Everyone sat. "Some of us have never been to a seder before," Marilyn continued, nodding overtly at Harris. "So we hope you'll feel comfortable participating as much or as little as you'd like." Harris, his face gone pink like a healthy vulva, looked down at his poppy, his thick navy blue band, his evenly spaced flatware. He wore his new *kippah,* which bore a Hebrew transliteration of his hilariously un-Hebraic name. *Ha-reess.*

"*This* is the bread of affliction," Kevin said, breaking off a corner of matzo and waving it at Harris. "That's all you have to know, bro. Eat too much and you won't have a bowel movement for days." Jason and Larry chuckled, and Harris nodded solemnly. In Joanna's head, the musical refrain: *One of these things is not like the other. . . .*

"Good to know, good to know."

Ron passed around his doctored Haggadot, myriad colorful post-its and inserts poking out from within. "Harris. Will you do us the privilege of reading us the order of the seder on page four?" To Ron's right, Harris's eagerness gave him the air of a magician's assistant. He nodded, cleared his throat.

"One. Recite the kaddish—"

Aunt Barbi giggled. "The kaddish is for the dead. We don't want to say kaddish anytime soon."

"Recite the kiddush, sorry. Two. Wash the hands. Three. Eat a green vegetable. Four. Break the middle matzo and hide half of it for the *afikomen.* Five. Recite the Passover story. Six. Wash the hands before the meal. Seven. Say the *hamotzi* and the special blessing for the matzo. Eight. Eat the bitter herb. Nine. Eat the bitter herb and the matzo together. Ten. Serve the festival meal. Eleven. Eat the *afikomen.* Twelve. Say the grace after meals. Thirteen. Recite the *hallel.* Fourteen. Conclude the seder."

Joanna watched him as he spoke. From Harris's mouth,

viewed from without, the seder sounded totally foreign even to her, like common cultural phenomena described in purely anthropological terms. A man's necktie was nothing more than *a long thin swatch of fabric, which a man must fold specifically into a knot at his throat if he wishes to be taken seriously in business; the failure to properly do so relegates him to a lower social and economic strata.* Who gave a shit in those terms? Who could tie a tie with any measure of importance or seriousness in those terms? Jesus, why bother? Getting a master's was reduced, simply, to *the ritualized study of a specific topic leading up to conferrence of inflated intellectual status by those who have already completed ritualized study;* everything was rendered meaningless and pointless from the outside, everything familiar and taken for granted canceled out entirely. So it was. A seder was: *Recite the kiddush, wash the hands, eat a green vegetable, break the middle matzo, recite the story, wash the hands, say the blessings, eat the bitter herb, eat the bitter herb and matzo together, serve the festival meal, eat the* afikomen, *say grace, recite the* hallel. That was all. Get too carried away with that line of thinking, however, and one might find oneself wearing the same underwear for three days at a time, dropping out of one's MFA program, and invalidating one's semibeloved family seder with one's unforgivable, covert, probable unkosherness. Joanna leaned alternately into one hip and then the other to avoid direct pressure on the insistent itch while her ugly plate hurled insults at her. *Pussy,* it hissed. *Cunt.*

When he was finished, Harris looked up at her. He was doing this for her. He loved her *this much.* What did one do with this kind of love? Love that did not bestow broken heirlooms or moot promises or venereal disease? One of these things was most definitely not like the other.

"We searched the house for *hametz* today," Ron boomed, winking at Joanna. "Didn't we, pumpkin?"

"Yes," added Marilyn, "so you can all rest easy. The house is clean!" There was no end to the inferiority complex wrought by Barbi. Historically they despised each other.

"So on page one," Ron went on, "we'll repeat the blessing we said earlier, when we burned the last of the bread. This second time, it's actually letting us off the hook a little, in case we missed anything when we did our search. Because nobody's perfect, right?" Again he winked at Joanna. He seemed to wink at her more often in direct proportion to how much older she'd gotten since the last time he'd taken note.

He repeated the blessing for all the *hametz* they might not have found, a blessing for the blind spot, the things invariably missed. Uncle Steve, obedient and entirely without social skills, read along.

"Any leaven in my possession, which I have or have not seen, which I have or have not removed, shall be as if it does not exist, and as the dust of earth." It was the second time she'd heard this today, and for the second time Joanna wondered if she wasn't glowing pink and fluorescent yellow and ultraviolet, if it wasn't totally obvious to anyone capable of looking, of really looking, that this implicated her in a hundred ways.

Where was the blessing for Unbearable Vulvar Itch? She flipped impatiently through her Hagaddah, squirmed in her seat and squelched the all-but-irresistible urge to grind her fist into her lap, a thousand red ants congregated in her crotch.

They did the kiddush and drank the first of way too many cups of sickly sweet wine, they passed around a big bowl and pitcher and ceremoniously washed their hands. They dipped parsley into salt water and munched like horses. Ron broke the middle matzo and wrapped half in his napkin for the *afikomen,* making a big show of it and smiling broadly at the "kids"—Joanna and Stacey and Jason and Kevin.

Back in the day, this had been the best thing about Passover. A Jewish equivalent to the Easter egg hunt. "After the meal," said the old "Pathways to Freedom" Haggadah, "the children search for the half of Matzah which has been hidden. The one who finds it is to be rewarded. When the hidden part is found, the two halves are put back together again. This is a sign that what is broken off is not really lost to our people, so long as our children remember and search." And on taped-in, blinding orange paper, Ron's feminist, postmodern, politically relevant addenda: a *midrash* about soulmates, about two halves of a whole reunited for the order of life to be complete.

The dining room table, so deliberately laid, was beginning to be messed with now, plates pushed an inch this way or that to make room for Uncle Larry's elbows or Aunt Jackie's inhaler. There were no children at this Seder; there would be no shouting, giggling, running to find the *afikomen* when the time came. She and Stacey and Kevin and Jason would be coerced into a mock search for the thing (which Ron will have "hidden" in plain view under the piano) and then be rewarded with something asinine, like a dime.

Of course she was going to have to ask the goddamn Four Questions. She was a jackass for thinking she'd get out of it, now or ever. She was an only child, she was the youngest cousin. It had been her job since she could read, since she could be trusted to make the table Look Pretty. How is this night different from all others? It's not, twat.

But when they turned the page, Joanna bracing herself for the indignity of asking, in song, at thirty-one years of age, in front of her *boyfriend,* with this bogus traditional wonderment, *what it was all about,* she saw that Ron had supplanted the traditional questions with something new, Xeroxed on fluorescent purple: *How Different This Night Is!* It was a statement, rendered with full shock and awe. How different this night is! She almost laughed out loud, because *this* she could sing, *this* she could relate to her own experience! An exclamation point! This night was goddamn Different, and in more ways than one! Question mark? *Feh!*

From her own precise location on the map of things, Joanna was going to tell them all how it was. No more asking; she was a woman now. No amiable, broad, open-ended, question-marked wondering! Listen up, motherfuckers!

"Joanna, my darling girl," Ron said. "Will you do us the honor of telling us how this night is different?" Harris wore an expression of overwrought interest, eyebrows raised, that recalled for Joanna the playground admonition to be careful lest one's face get stuck that way. She stared at him for a calm moment, then smiled at her father.

"I will."

The Living

In her backpack for Auschwitz, Shayna Markowitz packs the following: sunblock, a date-nut bar, her passport (it was just smart to have it on her *at all times,* her parents kept repeating, somewhat menacingly, when they saw her off), the required copy of Elie Wiesel's *Night,* and her own crisp, snow white, entirely blank journal (out of which she's thus far torn nine ill-begun, stupidly written pages and counting).

The morning is freezing cold, and Rabbi Amy goes from door to door, knocking them awake before it's light out. Knock, knock, knock, *Good morning!* Knock, knock, knock, *Good morning!* All down the hallway of the Hotel Continental.

"Today is Auschwitz," she writes in the journal. It is terrible that this will be her first entry—they've been in Poland for two days already—but nothing she's attempted to put down yet has been remotely worthy. She thinks for a minute, reads that sentence over, then goes on: "(well, actually, it's Tuesday, but you know what I mean)." But that won't do either, not at all, and Shayna goes to town on the binding and rips out the page, eradicating her pathetic words. Another blank page stares placidly up at her. "Today we go to Auschwitz," she ventures, but regrets immediately writing "go to" in place of "tour," which makes it sound eerily like a journal entry of someone in a cattle car in 1943, and which Shayna fears is sort of disrespectful.

Breakfast is a somber affair: some waxy bagels, rock-solid cubes of cream cheese, and yet more of the same pale, half-frozen honeydew they've been served at every meal.

"This is *so* nasty," says Jessica Berman.

"I know," says Jamie Ziegler. "I'm *starving,* and I only have like three Power Bars left." Shayna makes a mental note to offer Jamie some of her date-nut bar later, at an especially crucial, emotionally pitched moment. At the crematoria, maybe.

"I heard there's a snack bar there," Jessica says. "Seriously. I heard that." But then, catching herself—*Auschwitz!*—she sets her mouth into something of a grimace and loads up a plate without another word. It is the spring of their eleventh-grade year. They are bus three of the northeastern delegation of We Are the Living.

"How you doing, Shay?" asks Jonah, making Shayna's whole chest collapse and then expand hugely within about two seconds (the mysteriously linked words "finger" and "bang" ricocheting around, uninvited, in her brain).

Jonah is friends with Shayna's older brother, Max. They came on this trip together five years ago and now Jonah is back to help lead it. Shayna has been snooping around in Max's room since she could walk, and aside from a particularly sour-smelling, dog-eared stash of soft-core porn, her greatest find had been Max's embossed leather journal from his time in Poland, which she's read cover to cover a number of times. She knows whole sections of it, she's finding, by heart. So in a way she feels like she's already been here.

"Auschwitz," Max had written, "has changed my whole entire outlook on life. I will never be the same."

"Fine," she says brightly. She knows Jonah beyond what he knows she knows. She knows, for instance, that he had gone out with a girl named Carolyn, and had been much envied by Max for his ability to hold Carolyn's hand at Treblinka.

Jonah gives her a friendly shove. "Can you believe you're *here?*"

She shrugs, smiles, hopes he'll touch her again.

They had arrived in Kraków two days earlier, tumbling off the plane and into the airport like a bunch of actors playing refugees: energetically bewildered, much too quiet, the bloom off the rose of the trip already, their polar fleeces rumpled, their faces imprinted with the stiff folds of airline-issued pillows.

"Baggage claim *four,* everyone!" Rabbi Amy had yelled somewhat maniacally, counting and recounting heads. Shayna had been aware only of what felt like dozens of Polish eyes on her (did they know who she was? Did they know why she was here?), and wished Rabbi Amy would keep it down a little. She knew what all the Poles would be thinking: that there was a group of Jews at the airport and they were *loud,* they took over the space, they smelled funny, like the insides of two airplanes. It was so unfair, Shayna thought, shouldering her backpack and hitching her foot up onto a plastic row chair to double knot her shoelace before falling back in line with the herd: These people only knew about Jews in groups.

When the carousel at baggage claim four remained empty and motionless, Ari Freed had patiently explained the situation to Jessica, who seemed somehow to have become his girlfriend over the course of the flight.

"Things are different here, babe," he'd said, fingering the waistline of her stretch flare track pants, a wavy lock of his hair falling delicately over one eye. "They're not as efficient, or whatever." Then Jessica and Ari had embraced, fortifying themselves against the myriad cruelties—past, present, and still to come—of Poland. "I hope my guitar's okay, though," he said, suddenly, stricken. "Seriously."

Rose-Ling Horowitz and Jamie joined up with Jessica and Ari in a circle on the cracked linoleum airport floor, and Ari dealt them all cards. Shayna sat on her backpack and hugged her knees.

On the bus they took seats that Rabbi Amy—too late!—informed them would be theirs for the entirety of the trip. Shayna's was a window seat in the middle, on the right-hand side. Next to her was Zoe Fischler, who seemed nice enough but who had hardly said a word so far. Zoe's grandmother was a survivor, which Shayna knew because when she turned to Zoe to say "hey" that first day, Zoe had continued staring straight ahead, offering, only, in a monotone: "My *bubbe*'s a survivor." Shayna deduced that this meant she was not to talk to Zoe about anything commonplace, not to try and commiserate about what snotty bitches Jamie and Jessica and Rose-Ling were, not to intrude with the profane.

"Oh," Shayna had said. "I'm sorry." But she wasn't sure what she was sorry for. That Zoe's *bubbe* had survived? "I mean—that's awful." It was awful that she'd survived? And then, finally: "It's great that she survived." Zoe nodded sadly.

Behind them, in the last row, Ari had gotten out his guitar and, as the bus rumbled into motion, could be heard picking out "Blackbird."

Jonah was sitting at the front, next to Rabbi Amy, who'd introduced herself as "Rabbi Amy" and so didn't seem to want to be called simply either "Rabbi" or "Amy." She had sharp little features, lank orange hair parted sternly down the middle, and wore a crocheted lavender *kippah*.

"Welcome to Kraków!" Jonah bellowed into the bus PA as they drove out past the airport through big empty fields of grass. One kid up near the front broke out into claps and even a "Wooo-hooo," and Ari had just gotten to the line about how *you were always waiting for this moment to arrive,* but the rest of them remained appropriately silent, riveted to their windows as if to so many movie screens.

Shayna had never been farther than the eastern seaboard, unless you counted one trip to Canada to have Passover with her second cousins (which she did not, as it had involved only one jaunt to a local mall and otherwise had been entirely contained to their house). Poland, despite her deep familiarity with Max's journal, was a thing so far beyond her actual experience that she drilled herself to stay alert, stay aware, note the shape and hue of each blade of grass, each telephone pole whizzing past. To this end she had gotten out the journal, a pretty blue-silk-covered confection she'd painstakingly chosen from among dozens at the mall the week before. She clicked her pen a few times over the virginal white first page, relieved to be the younger sibling. There would be no one after her, no one to snoop around in her room when she went to college, no one for whom she'd be cast as unwitting guide. She wrote the date, and then: "Well, here we are in Kraków."

The words were uneven, though; it was impossible to write smoothly while the bus lurched along. Ugly penmanship was extremely hateful to Shayna, for whom perfectly rendered, heart-dotted-*i* yearbook testimonials were a virtue, a character achievement worthy ultimately of Jessica and Jamie's friendship, of grinning, shiny-haired, glossed-mouth snapshots tacked to a bulletin board in a future dorm room.

The words themselves, too, felt inadequate and wrong; the "well" distant and formal, the "here we are in Kraków" obvious. She had blighted her pretty blue journal with this inauspicious beginning. It deserved better. Something jaunty and adventurous, all-encompassing. Something factual but deeper than that. Like Max's, but *new* and *hers*. She tore out the page carefully, along the binding, and spent the rest of the ride ripping it into ever-smaller confetti, which she let fall, finally, into the nether regions of her backpack like industrial snow.

In the lobby of the Hotel Continental, Rabbi Amy had handed stuff out. They each got blue windbreakers (One Size Fits All), blue plastic name tag holders with attached pins, and blue binders for handouts, everything emblazoned with the program's insignia: a Star of David encircled by the words "We Are the Living!" It was everywhere, this statement, stamped defiantly onto everything inanimate. The T-shirts

Jonah and Rabbi Amy wore, the luggage tags they'd gotten in the mail two weeks earlier; all things material insisted on it: They were alive, all of them, really, truly, here, breathing.

"In case there was any doubt," spat Heather Golden at the cover of her binder that first night. Heather's mom was friendly with Shayna's from volunteer work at the Scranton JCC, and it was thus assumed that they would be pals, but Shayna didn't want to commit; Heather was Goth, the whole nine yards, black hair, black lipstick, black nail polish, eyebrow ring fastened with a little stainless-steel ball.

Shayna, in truth, found the We Are the Living accoutrements pretty awesome. Max's, when he'd returned from his trip swathed in such exclamations of Life, had cut a dashing figure for the implication that said life had begun in Poland, that he knew secret things, the knowledge of which imbued him with special powers, a special place in the world. She had been only ten at the time, and to see him get on a plane wearing innocuous jeans and a red-hooded sweatshirt and then get off another plane only a few short weeks later wearing the windbreaker and assorted accessories identifying him as The Living—well, she had been completely awestruck.

After they were outfitted in Living accessories, Jonah consulted a clipboard and handed out preassigned room keys.

Jon Abrams held his key to room 420 aloft, like a prize.

"Four-twenty, dude!" he'd bellowed at Aaron Weiner. They'd high-fived, laughing. Later they were escorted off and lectured by Jonah and Rabbi Amy, who had apparently freaked because April 20 was Hitler's birthday, and they'd assumed Jon and Aaron were referring to that.

"What are you?" Jamie asked Jessica. They both wore, on

that first day and thereafter, ultrachic, low-slung velour track-suits; Jamie's baby pink and Jessica's burgundy. Jessica's fit her perfectly and exposed a 360-degree band of taut midsection; Jamie could've stood to lose a few, and her band of midsection fairly bulged.

"Three-oh-two," said Jessica, looking at her key. "What are you?"

"Four-twelve," sighed Jamie.

"Fuck."

"You're with me!" Rose-Ling Horowitz squealed at Jessica, holding up her matching key. "Three-oh-two, baby!" They hugged. Jamie looked despondent. But still cute, Shayna couldn't help thinking, eyeing the track suit, the way the legs flared just so.

"Hey," she'd said, making her way over toward them. "Hey, Jamie. You're with me. Four-twelve." She offered her key as proof. Why Shayna had thought this might be good news was a mystery.

"Cool," Jamie said carefully, in a baby voice, all the enunci-ation scrunched up behind her cheeks, way back alongside her molars. Jessica shot Jamie a sympathetic but victorious shrug, hooked arms with Rose-Ling, and set off to room 302. "Sarah, right?"

"Shayna."

"Jamie," Jamie said, pressing her palm magnanimously against her chest. She got points for that, truly: It was sweet for someone as popular as Jamie not to simply assume that Shayna already knew her name. Falsely modest, perhaps, since Shayna had just *called* her by name a few seconds ear-lier, but still.

*   *   *

"What's up with the Rose-Ling person?" Heather stage-whispered as they stood in line at dinner, a meager buffet.

"Her mom's Chinese, I think," Shayna said. All the food was muted, colorless: bread, potatoes, garbanzo beans, white iceberg lettuce, boiled chicken breast, the ubiquitous honeydew, squares of flat white cake, white icing on the white cake.

"Lame," Heather concluded. "Nebbishy dad with an Asian fetish. Rose-Ling *Horowitz*? Fucking lame." The garbanzo beans were suspended in some sort of gelatinous goo, but Shayna scooped some onto her plate anyhow, realizing for the first time that she was incredibly hungry.

The reality of dinnertime was four big round tables with plastic tablecloths and free seating. Around one table were Ari and Jessica and Jamie, etc.; at another Zoe Fischler was sitting with Jonah and Rabbi Amy. A few randoms were at the third, and the fourth remained empty. There really wasn't any way around it: Heather it was.

The food was cold, all of it, even the cake and garbanzo beans. Heather got busy seasoning hers to within an inch of its life. "Two hours down, two hundred and twenty to go," she said, vehemently emptying a paper salt packet. "Mother-*fucker.*"

At the head table, Ari emptied a salt packet down the shirt of a squealing, delighted Jessica. "Motherfucker!" she echoed, giggling.

Later they had what Rabbi Amy called Where You're At. They went around in a circle.

"Feel what you're feeling!" Rabbi Amy said. "Just the fact that you're all here means you're amazing people. Not everyone could do this. I don't know that I could've done it when I was your age." Next to Shayna, Heather gave herself a slow pat on the back. Aaron Weiner went first.

"I'm psyched," he said. "Really, really psyched."

"Everything's pretty cool so far," said Jonathan Abrams, who wore a hemp necklace and nodded continually.

"My *bubbe*'s a survivor," said Zoe. "So."

Jessica spoke for both herself and Ari, in whose lap she was sitting. "We're a little freaked," she said. "But excited! And also? Can I just say? The food so far is really gross, and I don't eat carbs, so I'm kind of worried about what there'll be for me to eat."

"I'm at a place where I don't have to talk about where I'm at," said Heather when it was her turn. She had her We Are the Living! binder in her lap and was busy filling in the word "Dead" after it with a black Sharpie, the exclamation point serving as the spine of the capital D. We Are the Living Dead.

Shayna looked shyly at the floor and said, "I can't believe I'm really here." She looked up to see Jonah smiling warmly at her, making her feel calm, as if she belonged and could just be. It was the right thing to have said.

Back in room 412 before lights-out, Jamie flipped her hair over, fluffed it a few times, and whipped her head back up, dazzling. And then, with a little wave, she said, "See you later, sweets," and was gone.

Shayna looked around at the dusty fake velvet drapes, the filthy throw rug, the bunk beds pushed up against the wall, and the faintly humming fluorescent overhead. She folded herself into a cross-legged position on the bottom bunk, ducking slightly to avoid bumping her head ("Do you mind?" Jamie had asked, her hand already laying claim to the top bunk. "I'm allergic to dust and stuff."), and tried for a second time with the journal.

Here I am in room 412, she considered. Or: *Jamie's my roommate in Kraków, where we arrived this afternoon.* No. No! Too plain, too uneventful. Too standoffish. She needed a hook, a way in, a real beginning, befitting the scope of the trip, of being not only alive but the Living.

"The weight of what I am about to experience is intense," she wrote. "I hope I can do it justice for my own sake and for the sake of my people." But when she finished the sentence she spent almost a minute violently scribbling it out: It was Max's inaugural entry, from memory, verbatim. When the words were satisfactorily blackened she removed the page expertly, like the first, along the binding, and promised herself it was the last time she'd fuck the journal up. This was *her* big trip, *her* turn to Live, *her* journal, and she would not wreck it with imitative idiocy, she would not save for posterity her own ineptitude.

She opened up her We Are the Living! binder to the table of contents: Introduction, Schedule, History, Feelings. She skipped the introduction. Tomorrow they toured Kraków, and the next day was Auschwitz, where they'd spend the afternoon walking to Birkenau, doing the famous death march. Then Lublin, Majdanek, Bialystock, Tikochyn, Treblinka, and Warsaw. Then Israel, the antidote.

She skipped History.

Under Feelings was an essay by Rabbi Amy ("You're preparing for some of the most intense feelings your [sic] ever going to feel. Don't be afraid to talk about these intense feelings! We're all here feeling these feelings together!") and an Elie Wiesel excerpt ("I remember it happened yesterday, or eternities ago. A young Jewish boy discovered the Kingdom of Night. I remember his bewilderment, I remember his anguish. It all happened so fast. The ghetto. The deportation. The sealed cattle car. The fiery altar upon which the history of our people and the future of mankind were meant to be sacrificed").

Shayna reopened her journal and put pen to page, fired up by something. But just as suddenly it was gone again, whatever it had been, and her pen hovered, its blue-gray shadow hypnotic and trembling slightly on the stark, empty page. Her neck had begun to cramp, so she unfolded herself and stood up, eye level with the top bunk. Jamie had brought a mini-duffel and a suede-bottomed backpack.

Snooping had been a lifelong habit of Shayna's; sort of her modus operandi, the way she figured stuff out—the stuff no one would save you the trouble by just telling you. In Jamie's backpack were magazines (a *Teen Vogue*, a *Teen People*, a *Lucky*), what looked to be a brand-new pink iPod, and Jamie's own journal, a hideous pink-and-yellow thing with sequins. It, like Shayna's, was blank.

Inside the miniduffel were three piles of neatly folded clothes (including a whole *other* velour tracksuit, this one forest green with racing stripes down the arms!) and a canvas toiletry pouch. The basics were all included: toothbrush, toothpaste, acne wash and spot treatment, Berry Fresh body wash, a packet of pink razors. Oh my, and what have we here? A bottle of prescription pills. *Zoloft!* Shayna felt a bolt: the miracle of rewarded snooping, the thrill of knowing what she had no right to know, what no one knew she knew. Very interesting. What in the world could Jamie have been depressed about? Given the tracksuits, the in with Jessica, the late-night rendezvous with whoever, could there then be hope for anyone?

She counted out three pills, wrapped them in stiff hotel tissues, and stuffed them into a corner of her backpack's front pocket. She felt decidedly better, then, about standing on the lip of the fiery altar upon which the history of her people and the future of mankind were meant to be sacrificed.

The strange reality of Kraków was that it was beautiful. Spring had sprung, and the city was in bloom, fragrant, lush. Just the right temperature, with a little breeze. They spent the morning gaping at the intricate old buildings, the crowded Jewish cemeteries. Even the ghetto, with its big ugly wall, seemed like sort of a fun place to be: like one of those themed villages within Disney World where you could get your Disney passport stamped. The birds chirped ceaselessly.

A pack of Hasidic tourists shadowed them all day, visiting the same spots. The Living and the Hasids were mutually compelled to avoidance, however, as if in silent agreement that they had nothing in common. There was zero eye contact, despite the coincidence of running into each other again and again: at the yeshiva, in the ghetto, at the cemetery.

"Weird, huh?" Jonah came up beside Shayna in front of the Old Shul in Kazimierz. He could've been talking about anything, really, and it was weird, all of it. Poland, Kraków, the

Hasids, being the same age as Max when he'd been here despite being the prototypical little sister and feeling forever younger. "What insanity," Max had written, "to see the whole Jewish community eradicated. Their [sic] all gone now, and all these Jewish places are just abandoned museums." Next to her Jonah gave off a sharp crack of wintergreen. Gum. "Ghosts of Poland," he sighed, breath fresh.

"Huh?" She turned to look at him, noticing the hard line of his jaw.

"Us. We're the ghosts of Poland. All gone." He jutted his chin toward the empty synagogue with its proliferate plaques. Hasids and Living milled about, taking pictures.

"Can I have a piece of gum?"

He gave her one, and Shayna rooted around in her bag for a pen and a paper scrap on which to make note of this notion—the ghosts of Poland! It would be excellent, original journal fodder.

"Man," Jon Abrams said at Where You're At that night. "It was weird seeing those Hasidic people around all day."

"How so?" asked Rabbi Amy.

"Well, at first I thought maybe they were Polish or something, you know? Like maybe there were still Jews left here. But then when I realized they were just tourists, like us, it made me kind of angry, you know?" He shook his head. "Weird."

Dumbass, Shayna thought. Max had beaten Jon to the punch on that one six years ago: "How weird to think that now we tourists are the only Jews here at all."

"Yeah," said Robbie Altschul, nodding. "Totally." Jamie was sitting on his lap, which solved the mystery of where she had been the night before. She shivered, and he wrapped his arms tightly around her.

They met their survivor, Sonja, who would be accompanying them to Auschwitz. She had a We Are the Living! name tag affixed to her cardigan, which seemed pretty redundant, given that she had survived, that she *was,* in fact, still alive, *truly* Living. Sonja had been in Auschwitz; her whole family had died there. She had survived, she told them, her voice shockingly steady, because she had gotten a job as a maid for an SS officer and his family.

Heather wrote "euphemism?" on her binder and held it out for Shayna to see.

Rabbi Amy passed around a handout entitled "Guardians of the Past" and then they talked about tomorrow. This is what they called it: "Tomorrow." Not "Auschwitz." They were supposed to let it all flow through them, she said. Express whatever they needed to express. Feel what they were feeling. Max had feared the worst: not feeling enough, not feeling at all. Which would, he speculated, make him a monster.

"It's gonna be intense, you guys," Jonah said. "Really emotional."

Shayna raised her hand before she realized what she was doing, and all eyes were on her.

"What if we go, and I don't feel emotional *enough?*" she asked the group, emboldened by the sound of her own voice. Max had wondered similarly, so of course this query would bring Shayna the support and empathy of all and sundry. "Like, what if it's, like, '*Da-da-daa,* Auschwitz, whatever'?"

"Thanks for sharing that, Shayna," said Rabbi Amy slowly. "Anyone else feeling anything along those lines?" Jamie shook her head disgustedly. Others looked confused, horrified. Jessica, who was leaning back into Ari between his outstretched legs, playing with a lock of his hair, sat up straight.

"My *bubbe*'s a *survivor*," Zoe said incredulously, after an interminable pause. Even Heather, eyebrows raised, wouldn't make eye contact.

Then Darcey Feingold broke down, sobbing. "I—feel—the—opposite," she hiccupped when she'd managed to pull it together. There were sympathetic nods all around. "It's just so . . . intense!" Here Darcey let loose again, and Where You're At fairly disintegrated.

"We're all here for you," Jessica told Darcey, stroking her hair. "We're all in the same boat."

"It's going to be okay," said Rabbi Amy. "You're going to be just fine. It *is* intense."

"We'll get through it together," said Ari, giving her a victory sign.

"You are *so* fucked up," Heather mouthed at Shayna, grinning.

Rabbi Amy told them all to get a good night's sleep—"You're going to need it"—but they stayed up late, then later, reluctant to allow it passively to become "Tomorrow." People gathered along the hallway and in rooms with open doors, practiced their grimaces, said things like, "It's so weird we're going Tomorrow" and "Can you believe we're going Tomorrow?" Darcey was an ersatz celebrity, wan and pale and sniffling for hours. People took turns holding her hand, hugging her. Only Zoe seemed perkier than usual, holding court on the top bunk in room 410, telling of her *bubbe*'s narrow escape from the gas chamber.

Shayna wandered up to Jonah's room and knocked on the door. She would try to explain herself via estrangement from her journal—that was justification enough, right?—he'd empathize, say something wise like, *There's nothing new to be said about this place so just give voice to your own singular experience,* and then spoon her, maybe, for like an hour. When she heard "Come in," she opened the door to find Jonah and Rabbi Amy sitting on the floor playing gin. Rabbi Amy was laughing.

"Hey there, little Markowitz! What up? The lady rabbi is kicking my *ass* here."

"Hi," Shayna said. "Just wanted to say good night."

"Shayna is Max Markowitz's little sister," Jonah explained to Rabbi Amy.

Rabbi Amy lit up, took a better look. "Oh! Wow. Funny. Yeah, I can see it. Your brother is the coolest."

Shayna stood there seething, not wanting to get into it, the *How do you know Max* and the hilarious and touching anecdotes that would follow, the ongoing canonization of her brother, the coolest. Did they know how much porn he had stashed under his bed? Did they know how much he liked to torment the family cat? Did they know that, at Majdanek, he'd gotten a boner from physical contact attained in ostensibly comforting some girl named Jen Miller? Did they know he'd once given Shayna a concussion by hitting her over the head with the remote when she wouldn't surrender it in the middle of 90210? Did they know that he hadn't even finished *Night?* Did they know that on his breaks from college he could not be bothered to visit his elderly, ailing grandparents? Did they know that he called his parents "the Assholes" behind their backs?

"Okay," she said. "So good night."

"Night, hon."

"See you tomorrow," Jonah said, with a cheerful wave she could feel in her pants.

Shayna went back to 412 and got into bed with her journal. Jamie was gone, the social/sexual chips having fallen where they may. She got under the thin, scratchy wool blanket, clutching her pretty, blue, empty journal like a stuffed animal. Ow-Shhh-Wits. She thought about how familiar and therefore comforting the word was. As a prerequisite for the Living, she'd been through a class called Basic Holocaust at synagogue for the last couple of months. She thought about barbed wire, dirty striped uniforms, a yellow cloth *Juden* star, piles of skin-on-bones bodies, mouths hanging open as though gasping for breath or trying to say something, one last thing. She drifted off to sleep wishing she had a piece of one of those images to paste into her journal, that she might then be off the hook by simply opening to a page, any page, and pointing at it.

There's a bonus round of Where You're At after breakfast.

"Thank you for sharing that," Rabbi Amy stage-whispers about a dozen times. "That's a very important and very universal feeling." Even Heather gets in on the act.

"Honestly?" she says when it's her turn. "I was kind of freaked out getting dressed this morning." She's wearing her usual excessively scuffed combat boots, a black broomstick skirt, and a once-black T-shirt out of which most of the black has been washed.

Rabbi Amy works hard to present a face that's more

curiously amused than irritated. "What do you mean, Heather?"

"It's just really fucked up to think about being in that exact place, you know? With the same dirt and air and leaves and buildings and molecules and whatever. I'm just anticipating never wanting to wear these clothes again." Jamie is wearing her forest green tracksuit today, and Jessica is wearing a pow-der blue one, and this, from the stricken looks on their faces, is not something that had occurred to either one of them. Shayna thinks about offering to take a thus soiled tracksuit off Jamie's hands.

They go back to their rooms one last time, and Shayna grabs her backpack, holding out hope that her journal will prove a viable commodity once she's *there* (though she can't yet rightfully consider it "her" journal. It's just "the" journal, "a" journal, someone's journal, it doesn't matter whose, and since it's fucking blank couldn't be distinguished anyhow), that today's the day her very being cracks wide open and spills over for sorting through.

She swallows two of Jamie's Zolofts with water from the tap on her way out, and instantly feels fortified and capable of dealing. The third, she figures, she'll pop on the way back.

Outside, before they get on the bus, Jonah orders them to take off their standard-issue Living windbreakers.

The cold is different, somehow, from the cold at home. Colder. The wind whistles, the sky flat and endless. A few kids comply and stand shivering; most hesitate and look at their shoes.

"Do you want to feel what *they* felt?" Jonah barks, pacing. "Do you want to *begin* to understand what it was like to have to leave everything and everyone you love and be cold and alone and not say good-bye and never come back?"

"No thanks," Heather whispers.

Sonja the survivor stands along the edge of the group, looking absent but resolved, her name tag still, rightfully, proclaiming her aliveness.

Then Darcey starts crying again, and Rabbi Amy goes over and hugs her and explains that it's okay, that she doesn't really have to take off her jacket, that it's just an exercise, that we can empathize without necessarily going through the exact same things.

But Jonah stares them all down as if it's a dare. After a few minutes they go ahead and board the bus.

As they drive, Shayna sees the wooden railroad tracks all overgrown with grass and weeds, racing alongside the bus. She reaches for the journal, some fragment germinating about these juxtaposed, parallel methods of transport, about the busload of windbreakered Living on their voluntary way alongside crumbled train tracks to the death camp, but she vetoes it as soon as that now-familiar hovering pen-shadow appears over the white page. They're on their way to *Auschwitz,* idiot! Genocide, Holocaust, Hitler, Jewish History, Continuity. These are words that begin with capital letters, for fuck's sake. The stakes grew ever higher, and the fact that the journal was still empty meant that the opener needed to be especially brilliant. Lowercase thoughts—train tracks!—would not do.

Max had written a poem on the way to Auschwitz. "So Many Lives," it was called. "So very many lives were lost / of them all what is the cost?" it had begun. It was beautiful. He'd read it aloud to Shayna and their parents upon his return, and everyone thought that he should seriously publish it.

At the entrance is a sign in several languages. Before she locates the English, Shayna half expects to see a height minimum, like for a roller coaster. "The place you are about to enter," it begins, "is a site of extreme terror." Shayna finds it nuts that people might not know where they were. Like after being forewarned in this manner someone might go, "You know what? I'm not really up for extreme terror today. Why don't we go check out some kiddie rides somewhere instead?" Zoe, Aaron, and Rose-Ling snap picures of this sign. Jessica and Ari ask Jamie to take one of them together. "Move over that way," she tells them, shuffling her hand to the left. "Your head is blocking the words."

They pass by the double rows of barbed wire and under *Arbeit Macht Frei*. She's seen pictures of this gate; it's famous. It reminds her of the new mall promenade in downtown Philadelphia, which also has pretty wrought-iron arches.

"Shopping makes you free," her dad always says whenever they go there.

The parking lot is a mess of tour buses, and there is, indeed, a snack bar. The place is hopping. Vibrant, even. Shayna feels around for any feeling at all. It's actually not unlike the time she made out with Michael Rand in the tenth grade. She'd been way behind all her friends in getting that far, and had spent the entire nine minutes of her interlude with Michael thinking, alternately, *I can't believe this is happening,* and *Oh my God I'm making out with Michael Rand,* and *This is actu-*

ally happening right now, and *Allie says it feels like Jell-O and it's true!* So when Allie had asked how it was, Shayna found that she had no fucking idea how it was, and could only answer that, well, it was.

Darcey is holding on to Rabbi Amy's hand, hanging on by a thread. And sure enough, the minute they set foot into the first barracks/museum, she's sobbing.

"Did she not see the sign?" Heather whispers.

In the barracks are photos and basic information about when, how many, who, and so forth. Stuff Shayna knows in her sleep.

Everyone is paired up instantly. Jessica is clutching Ari, Jamie is holding on to Robbie, and Rose-Ling has laid claim to Aaron Weiner, who Heather claims is totally loaded. Jonah, looking smug and magnanimous, has adopted Zoe, and leads her around by the shoulders, *there there*-ing now and again.

The next barracks talk about arrival and registration, about examinations, about turning right or turning left, about life in the camps. This is more stuff Shayna knows all about, could recite from memory, and mostly she's distracted by what she'll write in the journal. She tries to let something penetrate, but really all she feels is nervous about facing the journal later with nothing whatsoever to say.

There is a promising twist in her stomach when she gets to the photo of the Auschwitz Orchestra. It surprises her; it's actually one she's never seen before. The thought of endeavoring to make music here. It's so sudden and—Yes! Woohoo!—intense that she almost reaches for Heather, but doesn't, just in time. When the feeling passes she's sort of glad not to have succumbed to the dominant impulse, the compulsory crying and hand-holding.

Upstairs is a room full of gray hair. This is what goes through Shayna's head: a roomful of hair, a roomful of hair. She waits patiently for the image to sink in and for some profundity to follow it, but none does. Max had written about wanting to throw up in this room. Jamie buries her head in Robbie's shoulder, Rose-Ling holds her hands over her face, and Jessica leans into Ari with all her weight. There are only the sounds of sniffling and sighing and breathing (which all Living must, after all), in-tandem footsteps. Sonja explains that all the hair is gray because it had been shaved after people were gassed, and the gas changed the color. Shayna catches sight of a long gray braid, winding its way through piles and piles of yet more hair. It is the second thing to catch her by surprise today. It's like a punch in the gut, and she holds on to the wall, dizzy. This, though unpleasant, is also exhilarating, as it's an actual, organic, vomitous experience, all her own. Never before has she heard or read accounts of a long gray braid, shaved off a dead girl's head after she'd been gassed. What color had it been? Was it there for Shayna to see and for Shayna alone?

In another room are piles of prosthetics and crutches and things. It smells like burning plastic, just as Max had promised it would. The roomful of shoes also smells, though Shayna takes issue, now that she herself is here, with Max's assessment of the smell as armpit. The smell is simply dank, fungal feet, any idiot could tell that much.

When they're done with the barracks, everyone is puffy faced and quiet. The hand-holding escalates to indiscriminate hugging. Everyone embraces and switches partners so that every possible permutation of couple has embraced.

"They're like swingers in suburbia," Heather says. No one tries to hug Heather, and because of her proximity to Heather, no one tries to hug Shayna either. And, needless to say, Heather and Shayna do not hug.

Most of them are wearing their We Are the Living! windbreakers over their We Are the Living! sweatshirts (or stretch flare tracksuits), and the sight of them, a small swarm of Living, all in blue, is truly obnoxious. It's as if they're gloating. Isn't it enough that they're here, at Auschwitz, alive, sixty years later, without having to proclaim their aLiveness so repeatedly? *We Are the Living, and all of you who perished here (suckas!) are NOT! Take that, you hapless victims! Eat it! Look at us, alive, you vanished people. If you'd found a way to emigrate when you'd had the chance then maybe you'd have something to show for your sorry asses, some grandchildren wearing two-hundred-dollar velour tracksuits and with excellent sexual prospects for this very evening!*

Jonah approaches Shayna and holds her for what feels like too long, so she's not sure what to do with her arms. When he's done he holds his face really close to hers and asks how she's doing.

"Okay," she says. He looks at her some more, like he's going to ask the judges if they can accept that answer, and then pulls her back into him for more hugging.

"You're okay?" he asks when round two is over.

"Yeah." But with every move she makes she gets a head rush, and when she closes her eyes she sees Max's words, wondering *How many people died exactly where I stood today?* And it's not until Jonah has embraced a squirming Heather and they've moved on to death row, between bar-

racks ten and eleven, to light memorial candles and sing, haltingly, the Israeli national anthem, that it occurs to Shayna to
say, "Um, no." To tap Jonah on the shoulder and fall into his
waiting arms and tell him that she is not at *all* okay, tell him
about the gray braid and the Auschwitz Orchestra and all her
preordained feelings and having to follow Max here, having
to have all the stupid feelings that had been felt before and
that had been felt better.

They have lunch before the death march. Rolls and butter
and Kit-Kats, which they eat in relative quiet on the bus. The
impetus to offer some of her date-nut bar to Jessica is gone,
and Shayna sinks into her seat and chews, chews, chews until
it's all gone. With her bottled water she swallows the third of
Jamie's Zoloft, closes her eyes, and waits for it to kick in.

"Help me find some good rocks," Heather says as they
walk. She scans the ground, bending down every few minutes to pick up a handful of gravel or a small stone, which
she then mostly throws back down, unsatisfied. "I'm gonna
make me a death march mosaic when I get home." When
she finds stones she likes she deposits them in a little plastic baggie. So everyone but Shayna has a trauma-assimilation
game plan, it appears; a way to feel what they feel, felt, will
feel.

They are a blue river of Living, winding their way along
the tracks from Auschwitz to Birkenau, on a most horrifically
well-worn path. Shayna digs her right thumbnail into her left
palm, grinding it mercilessly. Feel! Feel! Horror! When that
doesn't work she goes to work yanking out some hair at the
base of her neck. Jessica and Jamie and Rose-Ling and Ari and
Robbie and Jon have linked arms and walk as a unit, and

143

watching them, Shayna is filled with a burst of unparalleled hatred, the third thing to catch her by surprise today.

The walk takes only a half hour. They're greeted at Birkenau by more barracks, and the destroyed crematoria at the far end of the camp. Sonja tells them that the United States knew where all the crematoria were, and could have bombed them any time it wanted to. Shayna knows this, of course, knows all about it, but Jamie is incredulous.

"So why didn't it? I mean we?" No one has an answer, obviously, and now it's Jamie's turn to burst into tears.

"Because fuck the Jews," Heather says. Sonja nods slightly. "Kind of."

Sonja talks for a while about her experiences with a detachment that Shayna wholly appreciates but can't fully understand. How is it possible that someone could live through such things, then stand around calmly telling people about them? How is it possible for Sonja to be standing on this spot and still be breathing? Was this the secret knowledge to be gleaned? Was this what Max had understood and then alluded, in his journal, to understanding for the first time? Was this living with a capital *L*?

They light memorial candles, mumble their collective way through a mourner's kaddish.

On the walk back Rabbi Amy attempts to involve them in a rousing chorus of "Am Yisrael Chai" (the Jewish people live!), but the sky is threatening a downpour, and they book it back to the bus so as not to get drenched. It starts coming down hard once they're back at Auschwitz and the girls sprint to the bus, but Shayna welcomes the rain, wants to get wet and be made really uncomfortable, wants to be cold and damp and understand, finally, what *they* felt. And she gets what she wants, but only partially. When she falls into her seat next to Zoe, her clothes and hair are cold and wet and she's pretty uncomfortable, but there's nothing else there: no new, deeper understanding of anything but plain cold, wet, discomfort. As the bus pulls away, though, Ari treats them to an impromptu guitar performance of "Knockin' on Heaven's Door," which is very intense, very moving, and very, very sad, indeed.

Hotline

When the hotline phone rings it makes my shift partner, Miranda, and me both jump. I had a roommate last year who had the same exact phone, left over from the fluorescent eighties, the plastic cover see-through with all the incoherent mechanisms of telecommunication visible underneath. Its ring, shrill and indefatigable, would startle me in the most unpleasant way whenever someone called her, which was not often; she had few friends. It is not often that we get calls here, either, lately. Miranda and I and the rest of the counselors speculate on the reasons for this. We do a poor job publicizing, perhaps, or people are embarrassed to call their peers (some of whom they probably know, have classes with, see in the student center, glare at in passing, avoid altogether), or antidepressants have taken over. We sarcastically bemoan the apparent lack of desperation on campus. Kids today and all that. We are not needed by the people we want to need us. Like old, ugly whores, though, we have our regulars.

The ring makes us shiver in recognition, our senses in up-heaval, and then drops us back into ourselves carelessly, so we don't know quite what to do. There is always that rush-ing, *Quick, answer it!*, the scramble to remember our words, careful to present empathy, the breathless wanting to please: "Hello, Nightline." It is mellifluous and brimming with what we hope are comfort and ease.

Tonight when it rings Miranda is reading a magazine on a couch worn down by expectation. Behind her the wall stands indignant with amateur artwork: vines like telephone cords with sick-looking leaves and absurdly colored flowers, peo-ple's names, quotes. There are unidentifiable swirls and waves that look like whoever painted them just did so for the sake of it, giving up on anything concrete before they even started, not sure what they wanted to say.

I am sitting across from Miranda, slowly, methodically pick-ing stray hairs out of my arm. The screamlike ring yanks me out of my hair-pulling trance, but for a second I continue to indulge, unable to look away.

There is a panicked hesitation between Miranda and me as we rush over to the phone on the desk, a silent debate over who will pick up the receiver, who will quiet it. We decide, with shrugs and pointed fingers and nods, that it will be me. I feign competence, even to my shaking self, as I pick it up.

"Hello, Nightline?" I say it stupidly like a question. There is very little doubt who it is on the other end of the line. I am hoping against hope for a standard third party eating disorder call ("Hi, . . . um, my friend Jennifer? Well, she's kind of not eating? . . . And, well, we're all really, um, concerned about her?"), or maybe a nice freshman-depression call ("I just—I

148

hate it here, and you know, it's just . . . not like I thought it would be."). These I can handle. These I can offer some kind of service. Validation, Reflection, Referrals: our motto. Stephen, another counselor, likes to say them as an aerobic chant when the phone rings: "Validation, Reflection, Referrals, *whew!*" "Validation, Reflection, Referrals, *whew!*" "Validation, Reflection, Referrals, *whew!*" On the *whew!* he'll wipe his forehead in mock exhaustion.

But it is not a third-party eating disorder, or a freshman depression, or even a good old my-parents-are-making-me-insane. It never is, lately. It is Him, again, on the other end of the line, breathing His soft, heavy breath. The phantom release of air into my ear makes me flinch. Of course it's Him: the clock says 11:30. He's as consistently regular as a several-apples-a-day eater. We've nicknamed Him Fiber Man in a nod to His regularity. At meetings we all laugh politely at our weak attempt at humor and then lapse into thick, sad silence, thinking about Him.

"Hi," He says, hopefully. And then again, less earnestly, as though He is slowly deflating, "Hi."

"Hello," I say, lamely. I roll my eyes at Miranda and start doodling apples on the legal pad in front of me. She sits back in her chair and shakes her head.

His voice is enigmatic. Older, but so saturated with uncertainty that it seems juvenile; dense with a low-class Boston accent but slyly manipulative; full of shit but pathetic and open and raw. I wonder, every time He calls—which is all the time—who He is. Where He works, where He comes from, how He reconciles his habit of calling our University Hillel hotline nightly with whatever else He does in his life. I talk to

Him more often than I speak with my family. "How are you?"
He asks. My parents never ask.

"Fine," I say, although I am not supposed to answer Him. I
am supposed to remain silent and passive and let Him exhaust
Himself with no encouragement. This is supposed to get Him
off the phone as quickly as possible. (Another group joke:
"How long did it take you to get Him off?"—giggle giggle—
"the *phone*!??!" We relish our feeble stabs at jocularity where
He is concerned, they are our linen armor.)

I wait for a while, unfolding and settling into a familiar silence. Soon He will tell me that He is lonely, and I will say,
"Hmmm." Miranda is sitting back in her chair, still shaking her
head slightly, reflexively. *Join the club, asshole,* is what I want
to say, but I won't.

"I'm lonely," He tells me.

"Hmmm," I say.

"You know, it's hard," He says then, covering the whole of
his emptiness with a plush, vague blanket. I am well aware.

"Yes," I say. "It can be very hard." Then again, He may not
be talking about the living of His life. He may be talking about
His dick, enveloping it in His coarse hands even as we speak,
as if they were my female voice. I clear my throat. He always
hangs up the phone when male counselors pick up. "Life," I
say, to clarify, "can be very hard."

And at this point I want nothing more than to launch into
a monologue about myself. About all the disappointments and
the failed friendships and unrequited love and the crying myself to sleep and feeling safe only in the methodical pulling of
stray arm hair. *Isn't it?* I want to ask Him. *Isn't it just impossible to get through this life in one piece? Don'tcha think, mis-*

ter? Life sure is a bitch. What a pair we would make, the two of us, with our penis and arm hair; we could meander off into the sunset, mollified and finally fulfilled.

"Yeah," He says, drawing out the word like He's making a sweeping gesture with his hand over a barren and battered landscape.

The possibilities of who He is are so endless as to be overwhelmingly manifold and finally, *impossible.* Is He sitting in a La-Z-boy on orange carpeting from the seventies with only His shabby self for company, or is He calling from a mahogany desk in a room lined with windows, while the wife and kids sleep? Is He the bagger at the supermarket? A university administrator? Someone's dad? *Well,* he thinks every night, looks like it's time to check in with my girls. He unzips his pants and dials as if it were the most normal thing in the world, sandwiched between a late dinner and Letterman. The 'Who is He?' drives us all crazy.

"I saw Him today, in the square," said Jennifer once at a meeting. "He was caressing a pole and talking to it with His cheek pressed against it like they were going to dance." Or another time, when someone had gotten back an unfortunate paper from a notoriously harsh professor: "Come to think of it, Prof. Williams does have that accent, and I heard his wife left him." Stephen said he bet it was the glassy-eyed janitor from the student center, the one who asked all the freshman girls for their phone numbers, but Miranda told him that was just classist and to shut up. I don't say a whole lot in meetings, to any of them.

He sighs now, a loaded "Huhhhh . . . ," hoping I will take the bait. Miranda is staring at me. She scribbles a little note for me: "Get him off the phone! Someone else may be calling!" I nod as if I have every intention of ending this, but instead bite firmly down on His hook and ask Him how He's feeling right now. Miranda shakes her head at me again.

"Oh, you know," He says. "Frustrated."

Again, whether by life's circumstances or the mounting blood and pressure in His member, He doesn't specify. I offer another of my *I'm listening* noises and give Miranda a *Sue me* shrug.

All the other girls avoid talking to Him. A girl named Marisa had refused to answer the phone if it rang at His usual time. Eleanor and Rebecca both dropped out altogether, each citing some touchy-feely crap about taking care of herself before she could take care of anyone else. Miranda came up with a little speech: "I know you've called before and I don't think we can help you anymore. If you're in an emergency please call 911, Good-bye." Everyone agreed this was the way to handle His calls. Miranda is pointing to the words now, written out in hazard red stop-sign capital letters on a piece of construction paper taped to the wall. She draws her hand over her throat in a horizontal line, mouthing, "Get off." But I can't, or don't want to, or both. He is lonely and He needs me. *Me.* I gesture Miranda to back off. She shakes her head and jots down, "Have it your way, going to the bathroom." Then she leaves. I feel like an unsupervised child, justifying what I am about to do with the awareness that I was inappropriately left alone in the first place.

"What do you mean when you say you're frustrated?" I fairly whisper into the receiver, sheepish. I hope Miranda has to shit.

He is confused by my indulgence. "Well," He says care-fully, not wanting the call to end, "it's kind of like a build-up, you know? Like, I'm desperate, you know?"

His vagueness irritates me. I am trying to indulge this poor, strange man, and I want Him to be disgusting. I know He has it in Him, so to speak. The audacity to ask for a hand from me (oh, will the double entendre never end?) in releasing His frustration would entitle Him at least to a bit of my respect. I'm tired of people being too chickenshit to ask for what they need.

"What do you want to do about it?" I wonder, trying to nudge Him into the land of sweet, sticky honesty. I want nothing more than to be what He needs me to be, to make someone happy, to take the edge off whatever has led Him to us, to me. What kindness can I ever extend to anyone I actu-ally know? It is only Him I can help, only a stranger; only Him, a stranger who might be willing to ask me for something I can give.

He weighs my odd offer, dumbstruck, before answering. "Uhhhh—" His voice cracks endearingly, like a scared pubescent's. He lets out a laugh of disbelief. "Ah, I uh . . ."

I wait, poised to hang up if He won't be truthful.

"Could you, uh, . . . could you, could you maybe, um, . . . maybe just talk to me?" He stumbles. "Just, you know, talk? For a while?" It is only in His postcall, semen-soaked dreams that He has asked this of me, or anyone, before now. I think, in a flash that coincides with a glance at the door out of which Miranda has exited, about our little hotline group. I think about Stephen and Miranda and Jennifer and the rest of them, trusting me to answer this phone; about them having

153

bestowed on me the right to answer. As if I were somehow in a position to take on anyone else's troubles. And then, somewhere inside, I feel a ticking begin, a dangerous and loose ticking that gets louder and louder in my inner ear each second I don't hang up the phone.

So I do it: I begin to talk to Him, in a voice slightly higher pitched and more self-conscious than usual. I tell Him I wonder who He is, I wonder why He calls us, what His story is. I tell Him He should make friends, go out into the world and have it dirty Him like it does all the rest of us. I tell Him He should go back to school and become a therapist. I say for all I know He *is* a therapist; He is someone else's therapist, He is someone else's therapist's therapist. I tell Him I certainly know that things are not always black-and-white and that people are complicated. And I tell Him, in an overshot of compassion, because I don't really believe it, that I don't think He is a bad person for calling us all the time.

Throughout my little monologue, I can hear Him breathing hard, like a compulsive exerciser on a binge. "Go on!" He says, my captive audience, inflating my sense of civic duty so that it balloons massively—a true, red, beating heart to prove to me that I matter.

And so I *do* go on, with the assurance of being heard. It doesn't matter at all to me that He is not really listening, or that He is, in fact, using me. I tell Him that my name is Miranda, and to make up for the lie I start to tell Him other things, like what it was like when my parents split up, or why we had to move to Baltimore in high school just when I had emerged victorious as a popular girl, or how my dad married his secretary and my mom has no one but me. These are things I don't talk about, ever. Because they are mine, and once you give these things away they are scattered like useless feathers to the deaf wind of other people's empathy.

He is still letting out rhythmic exhalations that echo and imitate the beating of my heart as well as the still-present, inexplicable *tick tick tick*-ing in my head when I have exhausted myself of important things I need to tell Him. And then, like an old lover in sync with me, He comes just when I finish, at the same instant, with a gasp and a pitiful roar. We both sit quietly, spent, entangled in the fiberoptics between us. Dazed and embarrassed, I have nothing to say. It seems that I will never again have anything to say.

Miranda reenters the room and startles me back to myself as unpleasantly as the ringing of the phone took me away. She furrows her brow, jaw dropping in disbelief that I am still on the phone with Him. "This is not cool," she scribbles furiously on a pad. "What the hell is the matter with you??" I can't look her in the eye. She is poised with her hand over the phone, threatening to hang it up herself if I won't.

I want to say something as yet unformed in my brain to let Him know gently that I have to go now. But before I can speak He hangs up his receiver carelessly and easily, thinking nothing of it, with a click like the last tick of a bomb before it explodes.

We Have Trespassed

I was still doing my secret bleeding—a lot of it, and not the normal, dainty crimson bullshit either—when I deplaned, home for Yom Kippur and gingerly half waddling to accommodate my third maxipad in as many hours and the fact that I hurt everywhere. The cramps, as promised by the nice streaked blond at the clinic, were evil itself, and my boobs felt like two overfull water balloons with nerves. I was bodysurfing a weird wave of ache, my head heavy and hot.

My father gave me a little peck on the cheek, a chipper hello. He may have even called me "sweetie pie," but I could just as easily be making that up, wishing it so. My mother embraced me full on, which killed.

"You look terrible," she said to me, more observant than I would've expected.

"Not feeling so great, Mom."

"What happened to your hair?" she asked as we slammed car doors.

"I cut it off." Obviously.

157

"Yourself?"

I shrugged. It had been a very strange few weeks, indeed. "How's Lexi doing?"

My mother offered a sigh and looked over at my father, who managed somehow to stifle his own sigh when he replied, briskly, "Not good."

We were in a big rush to get home before sundown for the Last Supper, a feast of tofu steak, roasted new potatoes, asparagus, and salad, with fruit salad for dessert, all lovingly prepared and presented in honor of Lexi's having become a vegetarian, if you can believe that. The kicker, predictably, was that she wouldn't fucking *eat* any of it.

"Lexi," said our father.

"I'm not hungry."

"Lexi," said our mother, lilting, tight. "It's vegetarian."

Lexi, slumped miserably in her chair, tugged at a patch of hair at the base of her neck. "I said I'm not hungry."

"Lexi." Our father again.

"I'll eat later."

"There is no eating later, cuntrag," I said, trying to be amiable, flashing her an obscene mouthful of partially chewed potatoes. "That's kind of the whole point." I myself was beyond ravenous; I could not have been hungrier. Like I had a hollow leg or something. Only it wasn't my leg.

My parents had only just recently come (in typical delayed fashion) to a grudging admission that Lexi had some "issues" "around" "food." By the time I'd left for school in August (sweet escape!) there had finally been a slow meander through the Health and Body section at Barnes & Noble, a family visit to a special "food issues" therapist, a sweet if ineffectual attempt at creating meals she might somehow find more palatable, a monitoring of mealtimes that went pretty much just like this one.

For my Gender Studies seminar I had written a paper about socialized body-image problems and self-esteem, including for anecdotal supplement and sympathy a description of exactly this scene—my fifteen-year-old sister refusing to eat, our parents obsessively tracking her every nonbite—and my cool TA had written, "You poor thing!" in the margin, given me a big A- encircled in red like a plump happy face.

Lexi took a bite comprised of exactly two lettuce leaves and a nickel-size carrot round. She placed the half-loaded fork ever so delicately between her lips. "It's better to eat less," she said. "Then the stomach shrinks, and that makes fasting way easier." Her chewing was slow and exaggerated.

What could they say? She was right. And simultaneously she was involving herself with religious ritual. Genius. This was all going to make for a freaking *amazing* Gender Studies final paper, and I was even beginning to realize that maybe I could seek out double credit from Judaic Studies, maybe even combine the two to create my own major. I would go to office hours with my beloved TA, sit on her couch, tell her all.

"Fasting, Lexi, is not an option for you this year." My mother's tone betrayed a helplessness she'd been working hard to deny since forever. "You know that. We discussed it with Dr. Clayman."

No one seemed too concerned about the possibility of my fasting. I helped myself to seconds of tofu steak and refilled my glass, my appetite giving way not even a little. I had never, ever been hungrier. I couldn't get enough. The potatoes were warm and buttery, soft but not insubstantial; the extrafirm tofu had been marinated in teriyaki sauce, which gave it a nice tangy edge; the salad was fresh and crisp and dressed just enough (but not too much) in a light and cool tahini; there was a beautiful loaf of crusty French bread that had enjoyed a perfect few minutes in the oven. The medley of it all, rolling joyously around in my mouth and sliding still warm down my throat, made me forget, if only fleetingly, my unrelenting ache, the toxic sludge in heavy jumbo pad number three, and cramps so consistent I did not believe I'd ever be without them again.

Lexi had apparently struck some sort of deal with Dr. Clayman and our parents, stipulating a food minimum she was required to digest at every meal. I watched her carefully cut off a quarter of the tofu steak, cut that quarter into quarters, and then shave thin sheets off each piece, which she ate directly off the knife. Her focus was kind of beautiful, and I stopped shoveling food into my face for a moment to admire her for it.

"Five minutes," my father said, scraping plates into the disposal and then putting on his suit jacket. He refused to look at me, said my eyebrow ring made him sick to his stomach, said he couldn't stop imagining something catching on it and ripping it off my face.

Lexi visibly relaxed, another forced mealtime over, a long, blessed day of religiously mandated foodlessness wide open ahead of her.

It had been—I was 89 percent sure—my orientation leader, Peter, with the uncircumcised penis and ironic T-shirt collection and thick-framed glasses that served almost no ophthalmologic purpose. He knew *Pulp Fiction* by heart, and the oeuvre of the Coen brothers, and most of *The Simpsons*, too; whenever I'd had no clue what the hell he was talking about in any given situation I quickly learned to assume he was quoting. This meant that I was always adrift in conversation, clinging all alone to my immediate unfolding reality in a sea of arcane, nonsensical references.

"You don't win friends with salad!" I might hear in the dining hall. Or: "That Hanoi pit of hell," as we left the crowded mailroom. "Money can be exchanged for goods and services!" as we bought popcorn at the movies. "When Bonnie goes shopping she buys *shit*," while we strolled the aisles at Shaw's. "I'm the Dude!" pretty much whenever. Then, invariably, he would high-five someone. I had learned to giggle knowingly and proffer my own hand high up in the air.

He was a nice enough guy, a perfectly okay guy, but I was sick to death of him and the quotes by the end of September, right around the time I began to realize I wasn't menstruating, which happened, in the manner of all cataclysmic realizations, slowly and then all at once.

"My mighty heart is breaking," Peter said when I told him I didn't want us to get any more serious, that I wanted, I think I said, to be friends. "I'll be in the Humvee."

"What?" I said, and then remembered that we weren't actually having the same conversation. A week or two later, when I finally gave in to my insistent, shitty, unavoidable realization and bought an EPT, Peter had moved on to a sophomore from the next dorm cluster over and wouldn't speak to me, his mighty heart ostensibly broken, whatever that meant.

So I didn't tell him. And now it was over and I was home

with my family, bleeding. And not the usual dainty crimson bullshit, either.

Kol Nidre was its usual blur of the best in fall fashions available from Banana Republic. A mob scene. They had opened up the sanctuary via removable walls to the giant function hall, which was lined with rows and rows of folding chairs. Lexi wandered off into the fray as soon as we got inside.

"Amanda," my mother said to me. "Please keep an eye on her and make sure she eats. Daddy and I are completely exhausted. You have no idea what it's been like for us."

Lexi had never been one for role-playing along with any of my half-assed attempts to big-sister her. She dated guys older than I was. She'd had sex before me. She'd laughed in my face when I got my license and offered to drive her to the mall. She knew things I didn't. I was no kind of big sister at all. I had an overwhelming instinct to tell her about the sludge and the cramps and ask her if it was normal, if I would be okay. Surely she had already been through this.

The ache, temporarily assuaged by dinner, was back in full force, so I paid more attention to the liturgy in my *machzor* than usual, flipping through the High Holiday prayer book to find something applicable to myself, to the jumbo pads, the ache. I sat with my parents and followed along, trying to be what my friend Jen called "present." College had done this to me: I was hyperaware of a subjective reality everywhere, empowered by my newfound liberal arts curriculum to claim for myself, as my own, whatever the fuck I felt like. It wasn't, I suppose, all that different from Peter's quoting. I flipped curiously through my *machzor* the way Peter watched movies: essentially just looking for good lines.

"Where we have transgressed, let us openly confess: 'We have sinned!'" was a good one. And "Even the admission that we have done wrong does not come easily. How, then, dare we enter Your house, O Lord, Knowing that our failings are so many," was nice. And if I could imagine it coming somewhat sarcastically from the line-drawn mouth of Homer Simpson, all the better.

But in the *machzor* everything was stated collectively. We this and *we* that. We have sinned knowingly and unknowingly, willingly and unwillingly, publicly and privately. What a pansy-ass acknowledgment. There wasn't an "I" to be found. Not a single one. We have sinned without thinking, intentionally and unintentionally. Vague and broad and collective: What a load of crap. Nothing specific, nothing that directly addressed me, the sins I had committed willingly and unwillingly, intentionally and unintelligently, without thinking, my ache, my exponential jumbo pad sludge, alas. There certainly wasn't any *we* about it. We have trespassed? We have sinned? No: It had been me. My parents and Lexi, wherever she'd gone, had their own. The man swaying across the aisle, the one who used to give Lexi and me candy from his *tallis* bag during services, certainly had his own. There was, in fact, no simple *we* about it.

Outside the clinic there had been an old white guy in a rainbow lawn chair wearing a windbreaker and holding up a sign with a Bible chapter/verse number and a Jesus-fish-symbol thing (which couldn't help but remind me of Peter's penis). I had bestowed upon him the Indian name of Rainbow Lawn Chair. He didn't say anything, just sat propping his sign up with one hand and reading a Bible he held with the other, eating potato chips. I would have preferred that he scream at me, block my path with gruesome pictures of fetuses, call me vicious names. But he didn't look up from his Bible and chips, even when I paused briefly by the front door of the clinic, waiting for his tirade, wanting it, even, ready and willing to hear verses from his Bible pulled from context and hurled at me like Frisbees, one after another until he was plumb out and I could go. What was wrong with this guy? How was I to be dissuaded by something as simple and meaningless as "Exodus 21:22"?

I had, in the days following the clinic, been experiencing a constant hum of sorry underneath the waves of physical ache. And now here were these ineffectual, scripted *wes*, laid out in this *machzor* with our name and address stamped inside the front cover so I could conveniently exonerate myself via the universality of my sins. Not quite what I'd been looking for. It was a steady stream of sorry that no rote *we* was ever going to dam.

Next to me my father and mother were staring down at a *machzor* and off into space, respectively. There was a seemingly endless lot of standing and sitting then standing and sitting some more, and each time I had to delicately maneuver myself so as not to pass out from the scope of the ache and the vertigo of the sorry cadence rolling along underneath it.

I wasn't sure where these sorrys were directed. At Peter? At Rainbow Lawn Chair? At the whatchamacallit, an ovulation-gone-wrong, my itty-bitty swamp thing? It had taken on mythic significance, my own personal golem, a partially formed magic sprouted bean, an unknowable implanted as if by some sort of sorcery within me. When I saw Peter around

it seemed impossible that he had had an actual part in the cre-
ation of the bean, my golem, my teensy swamp thing. That it
was, most likely, his bean, too. Peter, wearing a T-shirt that
read "Fuck You, You Fucking Fuck," high-fiving his new girlfriend on the steps in front of the administration building: It
was his magic bean, too.

Could the bean forgive? Because according to the *machzor*
(and why couldn't this also have been John Travolta and Uma
Thurman sitting in a retro diner, shooting the shit about
Scripture?): "For transgressions between a human being and
God, repentance on Yom Kippur brings atonement. For transgressions between one human being and another, Yom Kippur
brings no atonement until the injured party is reconciled."

Right-o:

Lexi, I'm sorry I somehow always seem to know less than
you do when I'm supposed to be your guide, shining my big-
sister light on the path before you.

Peter, I'm sorry that I mocked your ironic T-shirt collection
and that I told my roommate about that thing you like me to
do and that you'll never have any clue about the existence
and eradication of the bean.

Dad, I'm sorry I don't shave my legs and that I wear jewelry
in my face and that all around I'm probably not what you envisioned when you thought about having yourself a little girl.

Mom. Mom, I'm . . . actually, Mom, you are a really
checked-out fucking bitch of a mother, and if you were nicer
in any regard maybe your daughters wouldn't have turned out
to be, respectively, a filthy whore and a snotty anorectic head
case. Okay, *now*: Mom, I'm sorry for having verbalized the
above. Please forgive me!

Easy enough.

Magic bean, I'm sorry—well, here I choked on it. Here I fell back into sorrysorrysorry. The bean fell between the cracks—it was not God, so it did not automatically forgive me, and it was not a person, so it could not be asked. I was fucked in regard to the bean, and I knew it in a way even Rainbow Lawn Chair couldn't have anticipated but would certainly have appreciated greatly.

You had to ask only three times. Forgive me, forgive me, forgive me. So why then were the sorries not stopping?

This was how I came to understand concretely that I would, most definitely, need to fast on this particular Yom Kippur.

It hadn't even occurred to me until just then that I could fast, that I might want to fast, that fasting was exactly what I needed! Why, I couldn't recall another instance wherein my needs and the dictates of my religious faith had coincided like this! It was totally the thing to do, and incidentally would add yet another dimension to what was shaping up now to be a pretty freaking awesome multidisciplinary term paper. Fasting was the only way. The bean was not God, and it was not a person.

And who knew more about fasting, not only about what it took to fast, what it felt like to really, really fast, but also about what fasting could do for you, where it could get you, how it could edify and fortify you and somehow empty you of everything at the same time?

I checked the two giant couches in the quaint and abandoned Bride's Room, forever the go-to spot for everyone under the age of forty on the run from services, but Lexi was not among the *Kol Nidre* exiles lounging on either of them.

Ephraim, the rabbi's son, however, was home from Wesleyan, playing gin with someone in the corner. Remember how I said I was 89 percent sure it had been Peter? Well. Ephraim, or E, as everyone called him (as much for his first initial as for his passionate relationship with Ecstasy) and I had had a sweet good-bye-and-good-luck-in-college bodily fluid exchange at the end of the summer.

"'Man-DA,'" he said. "What is up? You cut your hair."

I gave him a friendly hug and borrowed, at random, for lack of anything real I wanted to communicate, one of Peter's lines: "Yeah, well, the Dude abides."

"Totally," he said.

At home I changed into blessed oversize flannel and jumbo pad number four and took a Vicodin left over from my father's back surgery.

I knocked on Lexi's door, the house as dark and quiet as if it were far underwater, as if someone in another dimension had pushed the mute button.

"What?" She was sitting up in bed, reading.

"How's it going?" I asked.

She glared at me. "Fabulous." I sat down on her bed. She looked pretty. Too thin, of course, but you couldn't tell just yet that it was a *really*-too-thin kind of issue. At that point it just seemed as though she was just taking a typical crazy teenage girl thing one little step too far, emulating some fucked-up memoirs she'd read. I hated myself for not knowing what to say. An older sister is supposed to know things.

"You want a Vicodin?" I would hook her up. This would bond us.

"No," she sneered. Painkillers were *so* last year, I guessed. "I'm going to fast," I said. "I'm fasting, I mean."

She didn't look up from her *Vogue.* "Awesome."

"Got any tips?"

She paused and eyed me briefly. "What did you do to your hair?"

"I cut it."

"Go away."

I had no idea what I ever did to her. Truly, I didn't. Why couldn't we be friends? I had emulated some fucked-up memoirs in my day. If I had something to say, if I could help her somehow, if I had anything to give her, if I had some crystal meth maybe, then could we be friends?

"Lex, relax," I whined. "I'm hungry."

She raised an eyebrow and spoke impatiently. "It's not that hard. You just have to not want it." As soon as she said it I wasn't sure she'd said it. She went back to her magazine. "You look better with long hair. Close my door."

If I sat very still, which I did for a long time in front of the television after everyone had gone to sleep, I thought I could feel the evacuation of the bean, an emptying out, a slow, steady leak. I didn't give up hope that Lexi might come downstairs, watch TV with me, share some of her secrets of starvation. I got up for a glass of water and gazed longingly at the contents of the fridge, a bag of dairy- and wheat-free cookies on the counter, the plump teakettle. An overwhelming desire for comfort from these things, as palpable as anything I could swallow, briefly wrestled ache to the mat.

I fell asleep on the couch like that, a deep and drugged sleep, wanting a cookie more than I had ever wanted anything; more than I had wanted Peter just once to say something organic, personal, and middling, more than I wanted the *machzor* to feed me a line about something specific I had done and could then put behind me, more than I wanted forgiveness from the bean, more than I wanted to be friends with my sister.

Sleep was the only thing that kept me from those cookies, and when I woke up in the morning I'd bled off to the side of the pad and all over my flannel pajama bottoms, just missing the couch itself.

How was it possible that I could bleed this much and still be walking, breathing? What was the old misogynist joke? "Never trust any animal that can bleed for days on end and not die"? Was there no end to the sludge? The streaked blond at the clinic had told me all sorts of things I could hardly remember now about what to expect, how it would feel, how long it would last, etc. I hadn't been listening all that carefully, still waiting for that tirade from Rainbow Lawn Chair, sure it would come as I made my exit, sure I wasn't just going to be allowed to come and go as I pleased in that way, to and from that particular place.

Our parents told Lexi she could skip morning services if she ate a bowl of oatmeal.

"Do I have to go?" I asked, watching the two of them work together to make Lexi her breakfast. My mother cut up an apple, and my father sprinkled cinnamon and drizzled some honey over the bowl.

"You're an adult, Amanda," my father said, setting the bowl

down with a flourish in front of a sullen Lexi. "You can do whatever you want." Going away to school meant that I was an adult? I could now do whatever I wanted? They didn't care what I did? I was *that* free? Well.

I went. Stood and sat and stood and sat and stood again for a few hours. Followed dizzily along with the all the *us*'s and *we*'s.

And then *we* (yes, all of us, a collective unit!) came home to nap before the second installment of afternoon services.

My mother nuked Lexi a plate of leftovers, and the two of them sat at the kitchen table, acting out another version of the same scene.

"Lexi. Eat."

"This is absurd," she said, examining her nails.

"You're being incredibly inconsiderate, Lexi. *I'm* hungry, did you ever stop to think about that? And you're making me sit here with this food I can't eat. I'd like to go take a nap."

Lexi took a little bite, let her fork clatter back down, and pushed the plate away. "There! Okay? *Fuck*."

"Another."

Lexi rolled her eyes.

"We can sit here all day, Lexi. Please, let's not. I would really like to take a nap before we go back to temple for *Neilah*."

Sleeping, with all its forgetfulness, was the best buffer against hunger. I left them there in the kitchen, arguing over the plate of tofu I would have shot a dog for, fell asleep for what felt like about ten minutes, and woke, hungry as ever, with the sun from my bedroom window casting a patch of light on the carpet. The afternoon passed interminably while I tried and failed to sleep more.

"Mmmm, doughnuts," I kept hearing Peter say, Homer

again, luring me out of the library during those giddy first few weeks of school with a field trip to the Dunkin' Donuts on Main Street. I had been happy with our relationship, with how neatly everything seemed to be falling into place in this new life of mine. My roommate had accused me, snidely, of being a "boyfriend girl": the kind of girl who always had a boyfriend, who couldn't be without one, who wasn't ever alone, who'd rather be part of a couple—a "we," an "us"— than on her own.

But I didn't eat. I lay there unmoving in my bed, in my parents' house, and I somehow put nothing in my mouth the entire afternoon, even as the patch light from my window moved clear across the room. It was a tiny and victorious feeling, not eating, but the ache remained.

Alicia Ackerman, who used to baby-sit for Lexi and me, skipped over when we arrived back at temple for the last leg of services. I say "skipped," but she was like eight months pregnant with her second child, so it was really more of a sack-race amble.

"Mandy-pants!" she trilled. "How's college?" She grabbed my hand and put it on her belly, where she held it. "And Lexi! My God, you're so skinny and gorgeous. You look like a model." She kissed us both and kept talking. "You guys are coming over to my parents' for break the fast, right? Because you're not going to believe how big Michaela's gotten. And look how huge I am. I'm carrying higher this time because *we think it's a boy.*" This last part she whispered like a secret.

"I'm not sure I agree with you a hundred percent on your

police work, there," I said. (*Fargo,* idiot! High five!) Alicia rubbed her hand over mine on her belly a few times, confused. Alicia was, what, like eight years older than me? Under thirty, for sure, at any rate. She was married to the same guy she'd been with in high school, for God's sake.

"Of course we'll be at your parents'," my mother said, handing Lexi and me each a *machzor.* "I'm bringing kugel."

It felt disgusting to have my hand on Alicia like that. Like I was touching something exceedingly confidential, something that shouldn't be touched by just anyone. I pulled my hand away but too late: I officially had the willies. She was a giant loser. I, her former charge, surely knew much, much more than she did about the world.

Alicia seemed perpetually out of breath; a side effect of pregnancy, I wondered? "I can't believe you're in college, Mandy-poo. How did I get so old? Do you have a boyfriend?" She said the word "boyfriend" as if it was "cure for cancer."

"Yeah," I said. Lexi and my parents visibly perked up. "His name is Peter. He's a sophomore." I smiled serenely at them all. Lies, it turned out, were almost as comforting as cookies.

Our *machzors* were in a spate of panic: "The gates are closing!" It was enough to incite an emotional stampede. It was now or never. We were up shit creek if we didn't acknowledge some of our wrongs posthaste. We with our corrupt speech, evil thoughts, licentiousness, foul speech, foolish talk, inclination to evil, fraud and falsehood, bribery, mocking, slander, false pride, idle gossip, wanton glances, haughtiness, effrontery, disrespecting parents, and eating and drinking! And that was just today! And really: That was just me!

Hunger now was indistinguishable from the ache, and my

body was staging a weak revolt, a revolt that in spirit brought Rainbow Lawn Chair back to mind: slouched over tiredly, propping up his sign, engrossed in his Bible and his potato chips, not bothering even to lift his head for a fucking second to pass some judgment on me.

I mean, really: Fanatics weren't what they were cracked up to be. Even Peter, if he'd been a party to my day at the clinic, could surely have been counted upon to bust out with a Samuel L. Jackson–esque "I will strike down upon thee with great vengeance and furious anger those who would attempt to poison and destroy my brothers" or two. Or three.

"I don't feel good," I whispered to my mother, who was knocking her fist ritually against her chest, parroting along with the hundreds of other people in the sanctuary, the laundry list of trespasses we had committed.

"Don't be a baby," she said. "We're going to the Ackermans' as soon as this is over."

We had missed *Yizkor*, the memorial service, in favor of our naps, and I closed my hand into a fist and knocked it against my chest once, softly, for just that offense.

"So I guess this must have been like your favorite holiday ever," I said to Lexi while people swarmed around the buffet. I was waiting for an insult or dismissal, but she did the unthinkable and sat down on the couch next to me, tucked her legs up under her, laughed the smallest of laughs.

I was taking my own sweet time before picking up a plate and filling it with food. I needed another few minutes of hunger on my own terms. Not because it was mandated, but because it was over and I wasn't ready, like when it stops raining and you see people still holding up their umbrellas for a while. Now that the buffet was laid out before me, I could fast endlessly. I didn't need a bagel now; I could wait another minute. And then a minute after that, too. I could change my pad, I could take a nap, I could wait still longer.

On the Ackermans' coffee table was an enormous calendar: *What Does Our Baby Look Like Today?* Alicia's, bookmarked on day 209, looked pretty much like a baby, but I flipped the pages back to earlier, reptilian stages.

"Pretty freaky," Lexi said, looking over my shoulder at day 53, "Looks like a lizard."

My mother came over with a loaded plate, a napkin-wrapped set of plastic cutlery. She thrust it all at Lexi.

"Eat."

Lexi took the plate and set it on her lap. Her head held high, she glanced down at the plate as if it were China: far away and fascinating.

"Eat it, Lexi. Don't make an issue here."

"Great," Lexi said to the food. "Fucking great."

My mother stuck out a hip and stood there.

"I'll make sure she eats it," I said authoritatively, looking up from the book. My mother thought about that for a second, wondering if she could trust me. Then she nodded and hightailed it back to the buffet to load up her own plate.

We looked at the quiche and bagels and cream cheese and noodle kugel. A cluster of grapes. A piece of babka.

I had expected to inhale food from the buffet like oxygen, to ply myself with it, to fall back into it as though it were the deepest, thickest cushion net in the world, saving me from impact, to float away on the luxury liner of that buffet and live happily ever after. But now that it was here, now that it was time to eat, now that it was, in fact, *okay* to eat, food seemed not quite so miraculous. The plate in Lexi's lap was, in actuality, a simple plate of greasy quiche, a waxy, dense bagel, over-sugared babka, chemical-dusted grapes. What lay behind Lexi's fast, I briefly—and not for the first time—asked myself. Why was she not eating?

I scooted closer to my sister and slipped off my shoes, arranged myself cross-legged on top of another omnipresent jumbo pad, a corner of my thigh touching hers. On day one of *What Does Our Baby Look Like Today?* I saw something that looked not unlike the grape cluster.

Then I casually reached over, tore the bagel in two, dragged it through the cream cheese, and stuffed it into my mouth. I could no more have borne the bean at nineteen than I could have willed myself smaller feet or heightened athleticism. It simply wasn't possible. There was, as they say, no way.

Lexi gaped at me, surprised as I was.

"Really?"

The quiche was salty, and I chased it with more bagel, more cream cheese, more bagel. When that was gone I ate the babka, and then I picked at the grapes, stopping only to locate my parents in the crowd, long enough to see that they were over by the buffet, devouring their own break fasts and talking to their friends, laughing. I chewed and swallowed and chewed Lexi's food some more, a bottomless pit.

Lexi was amused and incredulous and relieved and probably a little disgusted, too. Her voice was full of wonder. "Thanks."

completion while you waited for me to continue spelling. *L,* you continued on, and then, again, a spot of bleeding, hesitant ink before the *i* and the *s* and the *a,* which proceed as they should before your slanted, rote, wonderful autograph. I remember being all too aware of the impatient line behind me, people clutching their copies of *Portnoy's Complaint, Goodbye, Columbus, The Human Stain,* the odd *Zuckerman Unbound.* I tried to meet your eye, I tried to communicate something meaningful. The others, of course, didn't *get* it. I wanted you to know: I *got* it. Later, when I found my way to reading the book, I actually purchased a whole new copy so I wouldn't sully my signed paperback. I cherish our moment of eye contact, your pen hovering over the title page, my name circulating in that colossal mind of yours.

But wait. This is no mere fan letter; no mere exercise in soft-core intellectual erotica constructed for your amusement. I have an objective. How old are you now, Philip? Early seventies, is it? You are, of course, notoriously private. I have the books, sure, like everyone else. And the reviews of the books, each of which mentions the notorious privacy. And there's the Claire Bloom debacle, which I hesitate even to mention, given its complete disrespect of the notorious privacy (though you might be happy to know that I couldn't find *Leaving a Doll's House* in any of the four sizable bookstores I checked and had finally to order it on Amazon). And *The Facts,* which I made a point of reading after the Claire Bloom, for balance. A graduate-school friend of mine was your research assistant for a few years while we pursued our MFAs, and it took her almost a year of postworkshop drinking to confess slyly, to a rapt audience of salivating young writers, her association

with you. (Otherwise, she was loyal; she professed total ignorance of your life, your private matters, even your address.
She seemed, in retrospect, somewhat terrified of you. I half
seriously offered her boyfriend a blow job if he'd get me your
address. The table of young writers giggled madly and took
big sips of beer.)

Yeah, so I'm a writer. Aspiring writer. And, could you have
guessed . . . ? I write fiction about Jews. Jews! Imagine that.
When I queried agents I categorized myself thus: "A
lobotomized Philip Roth writing chick lit." They liked that. I
had a lot of offers of representation. I'm almost done with my
debut collection, which has yet to find a publisher. And as for
the inevitable debut novel, well. That's a bit of an issue. I had
an idea, see. I spent almost a year fleshing it out, taking notes,
outlining, writing scenes. It was going to be so fucking great,
Philip; my God was it going to be great! It was a good idea for
a novel, a truly good idea, literally stumbled upon and embraced immediately as worthy of however many years of toil
it might take me, after half a dozen years crafting clever little
ten-pagers featuring women sitting *shiva* for relatives who
had molested them, women sucking their first uncircumcised
cock (then going out for bacon cheeseburgers, natch!), women
feeling left out and misunderstood at Jewish sleepaway camp,
to write a novel. A Great American Jewish Novel.

It happened like this: I was walking along Washington
Place, east of Washington Square Park, in the Village. A
block I'd traversed countless times before, only a stone's
throw from my apartment. It was early spring, still cold. I
came upon a huge pile of white carnations just piled—
heaped—on the sidewalk. Upon closer inspection I noticed

that each was affixed with a small sticker name tag. And then, for the first time, despite having passed it quite often, I saw the bronze plaque affixed to the building just above eye level. It was the site of the Triangle Shirtwaist Fire, the very sidewalk where dozens of barely postpubescent immigrant girls had landed in a charred heap after having leaped from the all-consuming fire, where now their names were affixed to ostensibly representative cheap white carnations. A hundred and fifty of them, Esther Goldsteins and Yetta Fichtenhultzes and Gussie Rosenfelds and Ida Jakorskys and Rosie Shapiros and Celia Gettlins and Annie Novobritskys and Unidentifieds, commemorated on the anniversary of the catastrophe that at once embodied and betrayed their naive, perhaps even as-yet-unarticulated American dreams. It was perfect. I immediately whipped out my oh-so-writerly Moleskine notebook (thirteen bucks at your local independent bookstore) and began to copy down the names and some notes, impressions of my oh-so-writerly wheels a-spinning.

I got to work that very day, March 25. I went to the library, looked around online, gathered information about the fire, about New York at the turn of the (last) century, etc. I put together a bibliography. I envisioned something grand, something all-encompassing, something at once contemporary and historical, intricately crafted to reveal a core of overlapping themes of American Judaism, the century-bookending phenomena of people falling en masse from tall burning buildings in lower Manhattan, my own rampant postadolescent malaise and fear, housed not three blocks from the site in a two-bedroom I shared with my fiancé until I broke my engagement and kicked him out a few months later. It was going

to be great. The potential was endless and unbelievably exciting. I was out for some Safran Foer blood, man. I would get a
grant, I would go to an artists' colony, I would sell first serial
to the *Paris Review,* I would have a stunning black-and-white
portrait taken by Marion Ettlinger, I would sell the collection
in a massive two-book deal which would warrant a clipping
in *Shtetl Fabulous* magazine, that glossy, much-hyped bimonthly effort to turn cultural Jewish identity into the
coolest shtick on the block, the new black. I could not have
been more excited, more—if you'll excuse the expression in
this context—fired up.

Anyway, it goes without saying that I love you. I first read
you in high school. (*Goodbye, Columbus*—don't remember it
so well, but the chick who played Brenda in the movie was
pretty hot, wasn't she?) I flipped through *Portnoy* shortly
thereafter, disgusted and bored. It enraged me like it had enraged all the good dumb Jews thirty-odd years earlier. I was
so idiotic, Philip. This, admittedly, had less to do with your
much-maligned opus than with the relatively few years that
had elapsed since the end of my own unfortunate, romanti-
cally unsuccessful tenure at a particularly vile Jewish sleepaway camp. All I could see in *Portnoy* was the specter of
those pathetic fucking Jewboys who didn't want to fuck me,
Philip. That was my tragedy at seventeen: No one wanted to
fuck me. My Camp Ramah might as well have been your
Newark, fifty years later and in Southern California, for all its
Jewish insularity and provinciality. The people with whom I
came of age in that pseudo ghetto aspired to meet, screw, and
marry one another (but not me!) without ever moving in any
respect beyond the psychological, emotional, and intellectual

ELISA ALBERT

borders of those well-funded, gorgeously landscaped sixty acres. They have motherfucking alumnae weekends, Philip. I get letters soliciting donations.

"Roth," I would spit contemptuously whenever the subject of your books came up, "Yuck." *Yuck* because in the defensively perceived *shiksa*-obsession and sexual dysfunction and casual dismissal of Jewish women and mockery of everything religiously, spiritually meaningful in Judaism itself, I was transported right back to Ramah, to being ignored and overlooked, to being made to feel freakish for my aesthetic, my sensibility, my desire for connection and friendship and love, to the weekly advent of the Holy Sabbath as purely an opportunity for us girls to look our prettiest and amass sexually explicit *Shabbat-O-Grams* from heavily-gelled-and-cologned boys, to the years-long, unrequited torment of a crush on a smarmy staff rabbinical student whose engaging smirks of dismissal I took as signals of subverted lust. *Yuck* because in Roth were Justin Steinberg and Eric Landsman and Ron Frank, those United Synagogue Youth fuckwads with their hemp necklaces and hackey-sacks and Phish tickets and body-hair aversion, and universal fetishization of Asian women. I didn't matter. I was powerless. I was overlooked. I had to hate you. I had to play that easy, tired "misogynist" card. Hating you made me feel better about myself—my Jewishness, my femininity, my mattering, the possibility that somewhere, sometime, someone *would* want to fuck me. In that way, of course, the trajectory of my (one-sided) relationship with you is not unlike that of the world at large, do you see? Because after some years of relaxing into myself and accepting my innate worth and spending lots and lots of my parents' money on therapy and electrolysis, after finding many men who did in-deed want to fuck me (who, in fact, wanted very *much* to fuck me! So there!), I could pick up *The Human Stain* and then *Operation Shylock* and then *The Ghost Writer* and then *American Pastoral* and then *Sabbath's Theater* and read you simply as the fucking astonishing genius that you are. Substi-tute the assimilation and success and general relaxing-into-the-safety-and-prosperity-of-the-second-half-of-the-twentieth-century of American Jewry for my own sexual liberation at the hands of (mostly) non-Jewish men, and there you have a rather interesting parallel in terms of our collective eventual appreciation of the writer Philip Roth, no? At present writ-ing, *The Plot Against America* is number one on the *Los An-geles Times* bestseller list. *Mazel tov.*

So. I am a young Jewish writer who idolizes you, cherishes your books, and reads them slowly, considers you the father of us all. Ah, yes: the father of us all—but not actually a fa-ther yourself, Philip, so far as I know. Why is that? Do you yourself know? Is there an answer? I realize that life is more complicated than that, but still, I wonder. Again and again I find evidence of child longing in your books. In *The Counter-life,* especially, our tenuous link, we find pregnant Maria aglow with Zuckerman's life growing inside her, the narrative changing and changing until she vanishes from reality, taking Zuckerman's potential offspring with her. When she reap-pears at the end of *The Facts,* she's still pregnant (more so, even), but there is no fruition, no birth.

And in *American Pastoral,* there's our man Zuckerman at his fortieth high school reunion, reporting (obsessively?) on the names and ages of his classmates' children and grandchildren. "I seemed alone in having wound up with no children, grandchildren, or . . . 'anything like that,'" he says. And one former classmate regards Zuckerman's reality with what I found to be the saddest two words in that whole tragic book: "Poor Skip." Poor Nathan, poor Philip.

Nihilistic Mickey Sabbath, too, adds his voice to this sad chorus, commenting on the fact of his having "never [been] blessed with children," and, furthermore, "children never blessed with [him]." (p. 326)

And what's that? Alexander Portnoy? Speak up! "Why then do I live by myself and have no children of my own? . . . What have I got to show for myself? . . . Children should be playing on this earth who look like me!" (p. 229)

Bloom, discussing your happier times together, recalls your regret that you hadn't married earlier, when you and she "might have had a child" together.

Perhaps it's my own baby longing that effects mere projection here. Perhaps I am just blinded by my own maternal desperation. I'm twenty-six, Philip. That must seem impossibly young to you—I am, after all, almost half a century your junior—but I don't feel particularly young. I recently broke up with a guy (the aforementioned fiancé) I thought I'd be with forever. I am the youngest child of rapidly aging parents who have no grandchildren. One of my older brothers is dead, the other is useless. I have a condition (thanks to the aforementioned fiancé) that predisposes me toward cervical cancer (no one knows this, Philip; no one except for my gynecologist and now you). I feel doomed. I feel done for. Do you know what I mean? Or do I seem shortsighted and utterly without perspective? I wonder sometimes if my pessimism in this regard is related to the despondent logic that disallows me from reading and carrying around and "wearing out" my signed copy of *The Counterlife*. No, twenty-six is not seventy-six. If all goes well (but why should it?) I have a great many years still folded unsullied before me. Books are for reading. Clothes are for wearing. Life is fatal for all of us. Sound wisdom, sure. But I feel ripe; I feel about to rot.

What happened with my fiancé, if you must know, is that he flipped out about his representation in my fiction. He looked for himself in all of it, and he found himself in all of it. He couldn't handle it, couldn't handle me and my big fat Jewess mouth, told me I was judgmental and ungenerous (translation: that I portrayed "him" negatively). I patiently tried to explain that those qualities are the very ones that confer any prowess I may have as a writer in the first place, and that furthermore I was *never going to get published anyhow*. What's odd is that I actually always took significant pains to disguise both him and his bizarre-ass family. But he couldn't see that. He found himself implicated everywhere, in every critically viewed male, on every sarcasm-laced page. He was a self-obsessed infant of the highest order (and here I'm not disguising him whatsoever, finally, but only because no one but you will ever see this). So even though he was also a big hot strapping Jew—and himself a highly successful veteran of my very own terrible Camp Ramah—I chose the fiction over him. Fiction is forever, Philip. I know you agree. Facts dissipate with changed perspective, reality is ephemeral; Viva la Fantasy! I chose my banal stories and the promise of redemption with my precious Shirtwaist Fire girls over a traditional partnership with a terribly limited man next to whom I'd lie awake sobbing at night, horrified by the stultifying limitations of the life I'd somehow chosen for myself.

I had been chipping away in relative secret at my Triangle Shirtwaist novel for almost a year when I found out I was too late. This guy in my workshop, AJ, turned in a story about an ambivalent Jew dressing up as Santa for a Christmastime gig at Macy's, and talk turned, in much the same way it always does, to the quality and quantity of contemporary Jewish fiction. A British girl commented on all the "similar stories" we MFA kikes persist in composing. She was, ostensibly, referring to all my ten-pagers, all my little Jewish-chick-meets-uncircumcised-dick narratives, to AJ's tired Jewish Santa, to a guy named Dante's Leon Uris–inflected action-adventures featuring Shin Bet.

"All your stories are the same," she said, waving vaguely toward AJ and Dante and me, we representative Jewish writers. This girl was working on a novel based loosely on the courtship and marriage of her great-grandparents in late-nineteenth-century Oxford.

"It does seem like there's a lot of this kind of thing out there already," offered a sweet Asian guy helpfully.

"Well, Jews buy a lot of books," I snapped, somewhat harshly.

"Yeah," said adorable Andy, my favorite, with a wink. "Jews buy a lot of everything. You have all the fucking money."

"There's a big market for Jewish fiction," Dante said earnestly. On one enormous bicep he sported an elaborate tattoo memorializing the Warsaw Ghetto uprising. "There are a lot of specifically Jewish book awards and stuff." The English girl looked annoyed, shrugged dismissively.

"I just feel like I read the same stories over and over again from you guys. They're great and all, but."

And then it happened. Someone whipped out a copy of *Publishers Weekly* and we conducted a brief poll, flipping through to informally count up all the reported recent book deals overtly by or about Jews.

Dante, hovering over the issue with the Anglophile, let out a manly squeal. "Jesus H. Christ, what's the Triangle Shirt-waist Fire? Some woman named Alana Orenstein just got mid–six figures for a 'genre-busting historical novel' about it." The word "FUCK," which as I'm sure you know is also an emotion unto itself, in all caps, just like that, crash-landed in my brain, in my heart, over my eyeballs, in my bowels. "FAH. UCK."

What else was I to feel? My whole year, my entire endeavor, rendered pointless. A waste. My brilliant idea, my literary jackpot, my huge undertaking. My Ettlinger portrait, my Vintage trade paperback, my Safran Foer smackdown: all sucked right back out of the realm of possibility as if by some mysterious, capricious, biblical-scale force of weather. Alana Orenstein was probably, at that very moment, sitting for Ettlinger in stark, beautiful, black-and-white half shadow. I'd felt something resembling this large-scale "FUCK" once before, years ago, when I first read Nathan Englander's heart-wrenching story about an *agunah*'s endless electrolysis and had no choice but to bury my own greatly autobiographical burgeoning novella about my own heart-wrenchingly endless hair-removal trials.

I numbed out. I let Andy take me out for a drink (read: five), and then I let him take me home and join me in my very own bed, surrounded by the dozens of index cards I'd put up on all four of my walls bearing the names of my sweet Triangle Shirtwaist babes. I had papered the room with them in an effort to truly live with them, those entrancing names: Yetta, Esther, Gussie, Minnie, Celia, Bess, Pearl, Rosie, Ida, Fannie. Quaint names, evocative of the old ladies those girls had not become.

Andy—"my favorite" because he is more than a man, more than a friend, more than a fuck buddy: he is my favorite of any man, any friend, any fuck buddy, and that, in a life full of men, friends, and fuck-buddies, is meaningful—blamed his subpar performance on feeling freaked out by the names, though it was more than likely that his six whiskeys were to blame. Or, come to think of it, the fact that my bed had been only semirecently vacated by that man I was supposed to have married, a man so "right" for me and yet simultaneously so heinously wrong for me that I can now hardly think of our engagement as anything more than a valiant attempt at arranged marriage.

Anyway, I didn't mind Andy's impotence at all. Fucking him was mostly an excuse to be just that close to him, to have him in my space, to feel his arms around me and feel momentarily understood, briefly gotten, in a way that is most rare indeed (somewhat like I feel when I read you, Philip, it must be said). When I'm with Andy I want, more or less, to wrap myself around him and crawl into a deep, dark hole with him and die with him. Have you ever been with someone like that? Amazing. The truth, anyway, is that I was too inebriated and distraught to be feeling genuinely sexual anyhow. So after that sloppy, comical effort at intercourse, Andy and I held each other (this is probably anathema to you, buddy; I apologize) and he passed out while I gazed drunkenly, dumbly around at those proliferate names, my Etta Kornbluth, my Dora Kirshenbaum, my Minnie Gluck. All still obviously long dead, but somehow even *more* dead now than before, snatched from me (snatched from the beautiful and infinite resurrection I was planning for them) by Alana Orenstein, by my own tardy, common inspiration. I had so wanted to breathe life into those names, Philip. I had experimented a little with their individual ghosts keeping company with my alter-ego protagonist (a twenty-five-year-old high school teacher by the name of Audrey Rubens who's just broken it off with her immature and abusive fiancé) as she traverses the sometimes-rocky terrain of her postadolescence in Greenwich Village. Yetta-as-patron-saint-of-marijuana, Gussie-as-patron-saint-of-alcohol,   Pearl-as-patron-saint-of-career-confusion, Minnie-as-patron-saint-of-one-night-stands,   Unidentified-as-patron-saint-of-the-search-for-love, and so forth.

There I was, Philip, all of twenty-six years old, my hard-won infant novel worthless, my broken engagement still haunting and heartbreaking, my parents still aging and aging and aging without the great reward of grandchildren, my cervix a ticking time-bomb, no health insurance in sight, my beloved graduate program almost over, my agent sitting on my collection until *Ploughshares* agreed to publish a story (read: indefinitely), temp-agency paperwork waiting for my signature. And the thought that kept me awake that entire night was simply that I could not find the strength within myself to start over on any count. Not on another novel, not on another stultifying relationship that might or might not lead to another engagement/marriage, not on any one of the many, many temp jobs lined up like dominoes as far as the eye could see. And yet I want the same things I've always wanted: a life of books and writing and writers, a second chance at rescuing and creating a life for those poor fucking Triangle Shirtwaist kittens, and a family of my very own. So here's the solution to all of the above, Philip; here's what occurred to me while I stared into the receding darkness that night, curled up on the edge of the bed to avoid the wet spot, Andy in a whiskey coma beside me, names, names, names on white index cards circulating in my peripheral vision; here's my objective, finally, the stage set: I want to bear you a child.

I had so desperately yearned to breathe life into those names, Philip. But now I've figured out an even better way to do that; a way to produce something literary and lasting; a way to prove, once and for all (while we're at it) the existence of God. I want to have your child. If I can't be the heir to your literary throne, I'd like at least then to be the vessel for the manufacture of an actual heir, flesh-and-blood proof, once you're gone and the books are all that's otherwise left of you, that you were here, that I read you, and that it meant something special, something singular and personal and only between the two of us. (The overtones here of traditional groupiehood and falsely-empowering femininity are hard to outrun, but quite frankly, and I hope you can buy this, I really don't give a shit.)

Okay, now. The practicalities. I don't want any money. I have a small, livable trust fund courtesy of my paternal grand-mother (whom I never met, and who invested cannily in the stock market, and who, it would seem, continues here the theme of long-dead would-be old ladies assuming center stage). My clueless parents, confronted with their only daughter pregnant by no man in sight, will surely help me in any way they can. Frankly, given the awful dearth of *naches* they've gotten from their three children (again: one dead, one useless, and me, trying now to make good after my spectacularly humiliating broken engagement), I expect full-on *bubbe/zayde* joy, the mystery of conception notwithstanding.

You can change a few diapers or you can be completely absent. You can watch her grow in monthly or annual or biannual pictures or you can take her to a Yankee game now and again (I heard about your big abandonment of the Mets) or you can have her up at your house in Connecticut summers. Or winters. We can live with you or near you or we can live across the country. I don't care. It can be strictly our secret or you can send a press release to the *New York Times*. You won't have to worry about a goddamn thing, Philip. I've got me some nice birthing hips (apple-shaped, like my mother's, which she claims makes child-bearing relatively easy) and I'll be a wonderful, loving, responsible mother. I'll grow roses and herbs and bake delicious vegan cookies. Send her to alternative day school alongside Hebrew school, sing her "Free to Be . . . You and Me" when she can't sleep, read her books and books and more books, disallow more than an hour or two of TV a week (but not in an arbitrarily authoritarian manner), teach her to be kind, generous, self-aware, inquisitive, ethical, shrewd. Laugh a lot.

The big question, though, is whether you still have the capacity for ejaculation. Did prostate cancer leave you the way Zuckerman's left him? Has cancer (or age) made, at long last, a cuddler of you? And if so (I know I'm grasping here) did you by any lucky spot of foresight (or optimism) take the step of putting away semen in some lab/clinic/whatever? This strikes me as something you might have done, you freaky old man. We won't get into the cosmic irony that may have wrested from the century's most unabashedly virile writer (that was not meant pejoratively) his power to orgasm, his power, even, maybe, to get hard. Isn't that just like the goddamn universe, though? Christ, Philip. But these technical matters we'll discuss later. Science is still pretty far from allowing a scenario where we might simply skin your elbow for some DNA, etc. But who knows? Let's burn that bridge when we get to it.

Anyway, your teacher and friend Saul Bellow sired a daughter when he was a good deal older than you are now, Philip. And no disrespect, but he wasn't half the writer you are. (Am I implying that he had thusly less of a right to procreate? That the world needs his offspring not as much as it needs yours? Maybe.)

I like Dora, or Celia. Or Etta. Pearl, too, or Yetta. Bessie's nice. And Rose. Minnie, I think, because of the automatic suffix "Mouse," would make her life fairly miserable, as would Gussie, for disparate, less concrete reasons. But I'll let you pick. I will send you the list and you can choose.

I can plainly see that you yearn, even fleetingly, for offspring. I can see that it's a hole. The longing is plain as day, right there in your work, in you like it's in me. I'm quite perceptive that way, literarily (even my high school English teacher said so!). There were all those abortions, all those near-misses (there really were quite a few, Philip, come on).

Your sweet and tender stepfathering of your first wife's daughter. You yourself were named for two dead uncles, and there's a pride in that, clearly. And I can hear the voice of Nathan's self-righteous prick of a brother Henry, in *Zuckerman Unbound*: "I *have* a son! I know what it is to have a son, and you don't, you selfish bastard, and you never will!" You knew just how Henry could get at Nathan where he lived, didn't you, Philip, because you invented them both? Well, fuck Henry. Fuck Claire Bloom, fuck Alana Orenstein, fuck Safran Foer, fuck the hipper-than-thou editors at *Shtetl Fabulous* who've rejected every single one of my retarded, inconsequential stories, fuck my nutbag fiancé, fuck my sadly lacking family, fuck, even, finally, Andy, my goyische, alcoholic favorite. Fuck the provincial, unimaginative Jews who made both our lives living hell for so long. Fuck cancer! Fuck the capitalist pigs who locked a hundred and fifty teenage girls into that fucking factory! Fuck the unions for not mobilizing until after the fact. Fuck death!

Listen. Portnoy had it right. What *do* you have to show for yourself, you stubborn misanthropic fucking codger? Children should be playing on this earth who look like you! Children should be playing on this earth who look like a lot of people, asshole, and life isn't the least bit fair. So do your part to make good on your existence while you still have the chance.

Because it's not too late. It's not at all too late! Until they put you into the ground you still have the chance to make something real, something alive, something no one can burn up: not in a stack of dried-out paper and ink, not in a grimy locked factory, and not even in a motherfucking gas chamber, you shriveled dickhead. Why would you pass that opportunity up?

A week after the Alana Orenstein bombshell—a week during which I did very little other than watch television, read *Star* magazine, smoke pot, eat candy, and sleep—I had the following dream: I was eight months pregnant, hugely with child, visiting a midwife for a checkup. The midwife, in full white-lab-coat regalia, turned out to be none other than Lorrie Moore, whose story "How to Be a Writer" (from *Self-Help*, 1985) made, at fourteen when first I read it, a writer out of *me*.

"Lorrie Moore!" I exclaimed. "Oh my God! I *love* you!" She was inspecting my chart and seemed unimpressed by my recognition of her. Then I had a thought, realizing that *Birds of America* came out almost six years ago. "Do you still write?" I asked. She looked up at me with those sweet sad eyes of hers.

"Nah," she said. "Not really. I mostly do this now." Then she went back to my chart before the obligatory, not (in dreamland) entirely unpleasant pelvic exam. (I have gone resolutely against the dictum of "write a dream, lose a reader" in this instance because [a] this dream really did occur! Truly! And [b] it's extraordinarily, perfectly telling, and I am just not writer enough to resist that. If you'd been born to ever-so-slightly different first-generation American Jews and raised on Long Island you'd be Billy Joel, okay dude? So don't be so goddamn hard on everyone.)

In the dream I left the appointment buoyed, as happy as I've ever been consciously, but as I walked (bouncing more than walking, on soft, rubbery earth) I began to hear the ending of that famous Strauss piece (you know the one—*Also*

Sprach Zarathustra, it's called, relegated now by Stanley Kubrick to ubiquitous diaper commercials and the like?). It was the ending, with its mournful group call and response: violins, harp, oboes, and flutes versus trombones, cellos, and contrabasses, which sounded to me as it grew louder and louder more and more like a *Please?* answered by *No* followed by another beseeching *Please?* and another resonant *No* and then yet another *Please?* until finally there are those three unassailable ending bass answers: *No, No, No.* It was my alarm clock, set to classical radio, awakening me. And as I came fully into consciousness I was aware only of those last three *Nos,* putting an end to my dreams, to my hopes, to that unconscious joy, evocative of the loss of everything I've ever sought: the novel, the marriage, the boyfriend at summer camp. And this too, probably. I'm not stupid. At most, maybe I'll twist things around and have a funny metastory with which to close out my collection, if it ever finds a home. And someday maybe I'll have some other man's baby, give her some thoughtlessly co-opted, vaguely ethnic, trendy name, write book reviews for my local Jewish weekly, lie awake at night marveling at the stultifying limitations of my life.

Kinky Friedman never had any kids. Maybe I'll write to him.

Fine. I'll just tear a page from the Roth playbook and simply turn this letter into a kind of postmodern "story" (and I'll even leave this part in to further confuse and complicate, to experiment with implicating myself, the "Elisa Albert" alter-ego, in all these ways you yourself are so adept with, see how it feels, how *you* must feel, when people assume fact is fiction and fiction fact, when people read your writing and assume they know you. Am I guilty of that, too? I suppose I am, and I'm sorry, Philip. It's just that I *love* you). I'll write it to Nathan Zuckerman from Audrey Rubens.

In an interview I read somewhere once, you speak of writing and publishing fiction as akin to packing a suitcase and then leaving it in the middle of the street, powerless to control its fate, its safety, its order, its intention, its meaning. And that's what this is. That's what any human interaction is, isn't it? "People are infallible," you wrote in *American Pastoral*. "They pick up on what you want and then they don't give it to you." (p. 278) Isn't that just what you meant? Anytime you seek connection, want something, make an attempt to explain yourself? A suitcase left in a bus station. So it is. I am the fiction; the suitcase is myself.

Yours,
Elisa

P.S. I'm enclosing a photo, because you're not necessarily known for your appreciation of inner beauty. I'm well aware that I might not be your "type," but aside from the occasional stray nipple hair, I am, I assure you, fairly okay. Points for youth?

About the Author

Elisa Albert is the author of the novel *The Book of Dahlia*. She grew up in Los Angeles and received her MFA in fiction from Columbia University. Her writing has appeared in *Nextbook, Washington Square, Pindeldyboz,* and the anthologies *Body Outlaws* (Seal Press, 2004), *The Modern Jewish Girl's Guide to Guilt* (Dutton, 2005), and *How to Spell Chanukah* (Algonquin, 2007).

Albert is an adjunct assistant professor of creative writing at Columbia and editor-at-large of jewcy.com. She divides her time between Brooklyn and upstate New York.

Turn the page to read the first chapter from
Elisa Albert's debut novel.

A fearless, arresting, irreverent, and outrageously funny
exploration of illness and death . . .

The
Book
of
Dahlia

{ A Novel }

Elisa Albert

Available from Free Press in March 2008

1. Something Wrong

Were there signs, willfully ignored? Did you know, on some level, that something was wrong? Did you avoid knowing? What were the signs? What did you know?

She had been having symptoms. Only recognizable as such in hindsight, but symptoms, nevertheless. A headache. Some sluggishness. Disinclination to do much of anything but hang around her house, take hot showers, slather herself with lavender moisturizer, watch movies on cable, smoke a bowl every few hours, make toaster pastries and consume them methodically, in quarters. Check her email, then check it again. But none of these things much distinguished themselves from Dahlia's normal state, so there had been zero cause for concern.

Well, concern, sure, but not *concern.* Just that her life was passing her by. That she might be, in point of fact, wasting her time, herself, utterly. That this might not be a phase. That, okay: What the fuck was she doing?

She'd figured she was due for a period. She always got those awful headaches, and/or the distended belly, bloat, and/or the general exhaustion. An impending period could explain away pretty much anything.

There was also the urinary tract infection for which she'd only just the week before completed a course of antibiotics. So there were all these things wrong with her. Not to mention everything, you know, *wrong* with her.

On the last day of her ignorance Dahlia Finger woke up shortly before noon, and ate a bowl of Cheerios in front of the television. *A League of Their Own* was on, for the eighteen-zillionth time, and yet again she found the thing totally irresistible, wound up watching all the way from Jon Lovitz's entree up through Tom Hanks's delivery of a tragic military telegram—pause for bong hit—and then straight on to the end, the disappearance of the young lovelies and appearance, in their stead, of riotous old ladies. By then it was almost two in the afternoon and Dahlia was weeping openly about the passage of time and the fact that Geena Davis and Hanks—so clearly meant for each other—never got it on, and the sun was threatening to go away for yet another day and so she made herself a cup of tea and looked in the magnifying mirror for a while. Then she called Mara, who was busy at work in Boston and, as usual, could not, or would not, talk.

"Do you think the Tom character just died alone and drunk?"

"I don't know, dude. I'm working." Little bit of judgment there, sure. Mara had, as they say, a life. "I'll call you later."

Dahlia's mother, upon meeting Mara fifteen years earlier, had refused to understand why this girl's name was "*mar-ah,*" which translated, in Hebrew, to *bitter.* "Mar-ah!" Margalit would squawk. "What kind of name is this for a girl?" Dahlia and Mara had come to appreciate this as funny and fitting. Dahlia always pronounced her friend's name with just that Hebraic lilt to it, because, she liked to think, Mara was just like her: a match, a true, bitter friend to the true, bitter end.

Dahlia had taken the GRE a few weeks earlier and was still resting on that semi-laurel: having (sort of) studied for and completed a standardized test so singularly uninteresting she might even have chalked up the headache to her brain trying to rid itself of useless information. The fucking GRE. Barely touched study guides still lay piled in a corner, under some health insurance forms and credit card offers she occasionally considered considering.

Why the GRE? Possibly social work school. She could consort with drug addicts, or battered women. The broken, the fucked, the totally broken, the irretrievably fucked. This seemed doable. Maybe she had a calling. Maybe she would be happy, self-sufficient, fulfilled, of use to humankind. Make her dad proud. She had just about given up on making Margalit proud, or even holding her attention for too long, come right down to it.

Anyway, the time had come to do something with herself. "What is your battle plan?" Margalit would often demand. As though life were a long fight one had to orchestrate carefully.

Dahlia had also toyed, intermittently, with the idea of rabbinical school. A pulpit would allow her to cast Talmudic judgment on people who pissed her off, and work on herself a bit, too, have an answer for everything. She'd be a cool rabbi, a real human being, a pot-headed, pop-culture-expounding Universalist. Except, goddamn it all to hell: Danny was a rabbi. Her douchebag brother, the rabbi! So the whole notion, over before it could begin, defeated her. Everyone already knew Danny, anyhow. They knew him as "Dan" or "Dan the man" or "Rabbi D," from his lifetime of camp counselor-ing and high school mentoring and University Hillel visiting and youth group shepherding: It was an insular, imbecilic universe, and Rabbi Dan, Dahlia's only sibling, was king of it. King Douchebag, Rabbi Dan.

Fine. So what sort of occupation wouldn't make her want to fucking kill herself every single godforsaken day? Law school sounded like a freaking curse; the words together (LAW-SCHOOL) like some sort of prison sentence handed down in a language she didn't speak, for a crime she didn't commit, by a totalitarian, undemocratic judge in a third world country. Too many rules, too much precision. *Laws,* for Christ's sake. Thank you, no.

She had no creative talent to speak of, though she had made a mean mix-tape in her day and certainly counted herself a reasonable connoisseur of culture (witness the umpteenth, slightly ironic *League of Their Own* screening, the bimonthly live music attendance, the requisite, half-read *McSweeney's* stacked on the floor by the untouched GRE study guides and untouched health insurance forms, indie theater movie stubs littering the bottom of her bag). She had attempted a spec script or two when she'd moved back to L.A. (because how could she not? She of the ecstatic, repeated viewings of every cheesy movie on cable during any given month's cycle), but they were derivative, unimpressive. One was *Sex and the City.* The other: *Scrubs.* Which she had never watched. But Dahlia's mean streak amounted to narratively unaccountable jabs everywhere: at materialism, stupidity, douchebag rabbis, dating websites. "Some fun moments, but way too hostile for episodic television!" said the only TV lit agent she could get to read the thing, the son of an old friend of her father's. "Why would Carrie stop wearing Manolos and decry the shallowness of her own fashion obsession? *Sex and the City* isn't in production anymore, anyway. Also: *Scrubs* is a hospital comedy, so it'd be advisable to set the show at or around the hospital. Best of luck."

It was a pain in the ass, this figuring out what to do with your life. A matter, as the famous book intoned, of finding the shade of parachute that best complemented you. But really: With no parachute at all you'd hit the pavement so hard it probably wouldn't even hurt, and you'd unleash a whole new color palate—bone, blood, muscle—in the process.

So screw the parachute, screw the battle plan. So weed and *A League of Their Own.* So napping in the breeze. So toaster pastries. So maybe social work school. Or journalism school (though there was the problem of facts with that one, namely a responsibility to them). So the GRE. Whatever. Things would "figure themselves out," as she told her mother. ("*Mah zeh,* figure themselves out? Nothing figures itself out! What is your *battle plan*?")

She was living her life isometrically: action with no movement.

This was officially a new start, at any rate. She had what her father called "options"; she had nothing but the time and freedom to explore them. She was twenty-nine years old and dear old Daddy Bruce had wiped the slate clean for her. Life in New York, never sustainable in the first place, had become downright unlivable. Bruce, bless his uncomplicated, wealthy heart, had offered her this out: Come home.

And, indeed, Bruce welcomed his little girl back "home" with a lovely cottage in Venice. He acted like this was Dahlia's right, as expected as hearing her Mirandas or voting. As inevitable as the bearing of arms. Of course she would have a house handed to her, a microscopic mortgage in place for her to pay (but only so she would "learn about money" and be "responsible" for it herself: he had a good deal of cash, but Bruce had "values" as well).

Dahlia adored the house, loved that it was hers (given, sure, but still). It was a haven, her very own airy bungalow box of clean ocean air. The Spanish tile, the stainless steel, the open kitchen, the recessed lighting, the beamed and soaring ceiling. To get to the front door you had to enter through a wooden gate and walk down a short stone path beset by night-blooming jasmine. She was going to go to Morocco and bring back colored lanterns to hang along this path. She was going to find a wind chime. She was going to get a hammock. She was going to paint the door blue. She felt safe, beyond the reach of all the shit that had dogged her in New York, in college, in high school, in childhood, in utero, and possibly even before that. She was anonymous in Venice; she knew almost nobody and almost nobody knew her. At night, in bed, if she strained, she thought she could hear the Pacific. She felt as though she was re-gestating; that for those first months she was rerooting herself via the cable matinees and pot, via late afternoons strolling Abbott-Kinney, stopping on Main Street for a coffee and a book or a *People* magazine. Watching movies (*Titanic, Flirting with Disaster, Mannequin, Thelma and Louise, Rushmore, The Goonies, She's Having a Baby,* it mattered very little) was a kind of prayer: She knew the characters as well as she knew herself, as well as she knew anything there was to know, and she could chart and rechart their movements and secrets and misunderstandings endlessly, reflecting in any number of new permutations on all of it, each time. Again and again. They were acquaintances—people she'd known her whole life and understood well, people incapable of letting her down by changing or disappearing or offering up the unexpected. The *League of Their Own* tears were purely for catharsis. When she was done she would reemerge, reborn. She would make new mistakes. Or maybe none at all.

Okay, wait. Honestly? It wasn't *A League of Their Own*. It was actually *Terms of Endearment,* but that just seems too easy, a bit ridiculous. Reality's fucked like that. That on the last day of her innocence Dahlia Finger could be found sobbing on her couch, baked out of her head at 2 o'clock in the afternoon, watching *Terms of* freaking *Endearment*!?

What did you know before you knew?

No, let's just say it was *A League of Their Own.*

(But it wasn't.)

On some level you may not feel surprised. On some level you may have known Something was Wrong.

Anyway, the symptoms. Clear in hindsight, so obvious once their root cause is known. A headache, sluggishness, disinclination. She was tired, but she had done nothing whatsoever to tire herself. It was somehow perfectly acceptable as the result of— one could assume—having no direction, no desire to do anything but sit right where she was, crying, feeling *something* at least (even if it was about Debra goddamned Winger) in her perfect bungalow, the salty breeze fluffing her white curtains— curtains she had hung by herself!—just so. Bruce had been excessively proud of the curtains, and of Dahlia for having hung them all by herself. Bruce was excessively proud, always, of everything. The headache, et al., spoke only to the uselessness of

Dahlia's existence—a life so relatively blessed and easy and boun-tiful that some festering guilt had to be thrown into the mix as well. Which quite plausibly added up to a consistent low-grade headache and the tendency to stretch out on the couch, stoned, napping in the breeze.

"Spoiled," she could hear Margalit spitting at her, running commentary. "Everything is too easy for you. You should have some real problems. You should know what real problems *are*."

Ben, the guy she'd been sleeping with, had wanted to get together that night for dinner, a movie, a drink, but Dahlia was happy on her couch, happy with her movies, happy with her weed. Ben exhausted her (like jobs exhausted her, like the GRE exhausted her, like her period exhausted her, like depositing Daddy's checks exhausted her, like going to the post office for stamps to pay bills with money she'd been given, no strings attached, exhausted her).

Dahlia and Ben had met at a bar party about a month earlier, a birthday of friends of friends of friends, on one of the unique evenings on which Dahlia had forsaken the couch, the weed, the movies, for a night out. A girl needed a night out every so often, and the infrequency of those nights out ensured Dahlia's total enjoyment of them. She was the life of the party on those unique evenings. Why didn't she go out more often, she asked herself. Ben was getting his PhD in art history, bless his unemployable heart. He confessed to Dahlia that he didn't get out much, him-self. He was the kind of guy she could easily imagine having had a crush on as an undergraduate, a goofy grad student with broad shoulders and thick, floppy hair, a messenger bag. If nothing else, imagining him as the object of someone *else's* undergraduate lust was attractive enough, and sealed the deal. She herself had never had the privilege of defilement by an academic superior. They kissed in the parking lot, his nervous smile endearing as hell, and his soft hands around her face like he actually meant the kiss. It was Santa Monica cold, the air wet and crisp. After

New York Dahlia had promised herself, as an experiment: no more fucking on first meeting. Could she do it? Ben was sweet-smelling and cute and those soft hands held her face neither too loosely nor too insistently: Could she make it to a second meeting? No, she could not.

"Follow me," she told him before getting into her car. The shy, delighted look on his face briefly made her want to change her mind, but it was too late. Fuck it. Life, as they say, was short.

But over a month later, enough! She hadn't wanted a flipping boyfriend, for god's sake. She didn't want to hurt the sweet would-be-professor, but really. "*Dayenu,*" as Margalit would say when she was done with one of her men: *it would have been enough.*

This Ben character was so eager to spend time with her, to be her boyfriend, to see her on nights like this for dinner, a drink. Who had the energy? The fun part was meeting them, playing the does-he-really-like-me game, finding out what they were like in bed, getting comfortable enough to relax; after that they could go away. Usually this scenario ran itself out on about a three-week course. Don't get too attached to me, she wished she could somehow broadcast to the poor guy, I have no interest in being your girlfriend. And you might not realize it, but you have no interest in being my boyfriend. Have a nice life, etc.

By way of excuse, and in what turned out to be a fortuitous twist, Dahlia had told Ben she wasn't feeling well, that she would be at home that night, hanging out, lying low, "taking it easy."

"Okay," he'd said, sounding defeated. Surely he knew the jig was up; surely he knew she was blowing him off. She hadn't made any real effort to spend time with him in over a week, now. "Feel better. I'll call to check up on you later."

Don't, she almost said.

And as the afternoon gave way to evening Dahlia was a little confused: She really *wasn't* feeling so hot. Was this her punishment? Had her excuse made itself manifest? Because she really wasn't feeling so hot. Oh, well. She made herself a snack bounty (Brie, a sliced Fuji apple, garlic crackers, Oreos), arranged it buffet-style on her coffee table, and settled back into the couch for another bong hit. (Would it be over-the-top to mention that *Dying Young* was on cable? Probably. So let's split the difference and say it was *Steel Magnolias,* shall we? A Julia Roberts/untimely-death compromise; how's that?)

It is only natural to revisit the moment things went wrong, the moment our lives went from okay to not okay, from normal to problematic.

The last thing Dahlia remembered was taking a break from the movies to watch an *I Love the 90's* marathon on VH1.

She'd put a frozen pizza in the oven, made herself another cup of tea, flopped down on the couch, and begun the long process of psyching herself up for bedtime: the always depressing end to another failed day. But there she still was, after midnight, letting first 1993 and then 1994 and 1995 pass her by.

And then she had a grand mal seizure.